AN ECHO OF JUSTICE

AN ECHO OF JUSTICE

Hugh Miller

St. Martin's Press
New York

MYS.

Library of Congress Cataloging-in-Publication Data

Miller, Hugh.
    An echo of justice / Hugh Miller.
      p.   cm.
    ISBN 0-312-06343-1
    I. Title.
  PR6063.I373E27   1991
  823'.914—dc20   91-19690
                                                      CIP

First published in Great Britain by Victor Gollancz Limited.

First U.S. Edition: September 1991
10 9 8 7 6 5 4 3 2 1

For dear Nettie,
and for
Jim Leslie

ONE

It was like when he was a kid. Steve felt young now and very small again. Small and easy to hurt. *God oh Jesus, Mum . . .* He let out some of the fear on a whimper. The noise it made in the empty house startled him. He pulled his knees tight to his chest and shuffled his buttocks closer to the angle of the walls. The crucifix dangled across his knuckles. He stared at it, watched light sparking on the beaded chain. It was night outside but everything was still too bright. There wasn't enough dark to hide him.

Hiding wasn't possible. Not the kind that made him feel invisible when he was a kid. They could find him here. Or anywhere, now he was grown up.

He had run to this place without thinking. In the days when people lived on the estate, Steve played in its streets. Nowadays the Thrushbush Development was a ghost of old times. There were maybe a hundred prefabs, vacated years ago and vandalised, scheduled for demolition if the council could ever find a buyer for the land. This house had been rented by the Jamiesons, an Irish family with a daughter Steve had adored when he was fourteen. Ages ago. Everything before tonight was ages ago.

Getting here, desperate to find a way out of the calamity he'd made, he saw a man and woman fucking at the side of a dead house like this one. Before tonight a sight like that would have put him into a reflex crouch and he would have found a peeper's shadow, double quick. Tonight it had been like hurrying past something remote and bizarre, the girl an upturned Y, her pale legs bracketing the man as he hunched and groaned.

Then and now, only Steve's fear was real. He didn't recall getting into the house, or how he'd crept between the pile of rotten

7

carpet and the corner. He knew he had pissed himself but couldn't remember doing that, either.

He shivered and tried to think of a bright side. His mother was forever saying there was a bright side to everything, all you had to do was look for it. Nothing was completely bad or hopeless, she said. The worst things, the very worst, still weren't *too* bad, because there was the consolation of Our Lady, who would forgive all sins and never withhold her comfort. But Steve couldn't feel her consolation tonight. He felt fear and he felt a shivery nausea that was part of the fear. And he felt lost.

The thing that had happened, the disastrous thing that had sent him running for cover, was blindingly vivid in his mind. But all the bright detail was unreal. He had been catapulted out of his pattern and only the fear had come with him. He wasn't what he had been earlier, when he left the house and put safety behind him for good.

'Hail Mary full of grace, blessed is the fruit of thy womb, Jesus . . .'

He gagged through the words and ducked his head, snuffling, chewing the beads of the crucifix to hurt himself out of the clutching panic.

'Mum, *Mum* . . .'

He shifted and his fingers brushed a patch of blood on his jacket. The cold stickiness sent his hand to his mouth again, shutting off a whimper.

TWO

When Superintendent Foster had to deal with the press, or with other important people, he wore a bespoke uniform made by a military tailor in London. He wore it tonight. The styling conformed with regulations, but it didn't look like any other police superintendent's uniform. The material was high-grade wool mixed with enough artificial fibre to make the folds look as if an art director had put them there. The braid and buttons didn't shine like regulation issue — they glittered. The cap, shoulders and lapels were braided with gold-plated wire. The original Sta-Brite coating of the buttons had been chemically stripped off before they were re-plated with 22-carat gold and lacquered.

'The big cunt looks like a Christmas tree,' Albert Coker said.

Albert's remarks were few and always spare. He never felt there was much worth saying and when anything was, he made his point with economy. A lifelong asthmatic, he had worked in the city mortuary for thirty-eight of his sixty years. He believed that long silences and the undemanding work of an attendant kept his seizures to a minimum.

Albert and his mate Davie wheeled a steel trolley to the side of the dissection table. Superintendent Foster watched them from the other end of the room, more interested in their cargo than in anything they might have to say. As Albert Coker whipped the sheet off the body the superintendent creased his eyes and turned to Detective Inspector Mike Fletcher.

'Ghastly,' he said.

Mike glanced at the body. The dead man wore a police sergeant's uniform. His face was paving-stone grey. The eyes were half-open

9

and dreamy looking. Dried blood was caked on his mouth and nostrils.

'It shouldn't take long,' the superintendent said. 'There's nothing to work out. We know who we want and we've enough witnesses to put him away twice and a bit. Ring me at home when you bring McMillan in.'

Mike was still looking at the body.

'If young Steve's got any sense,' he said, 'he'll have topped himself by now.' He turned his weary eyes to the superintendent. 'The righteous wrath of the uniformed branch could be a fate worse than death.'

Foster stared at him.

'Would you blame them?'

'You know I would,' Mike said.

'For God's sake . . .'

'CID's getting het-up about this one, too. DS Cullen's already said he wants five minutes on his own with McMillan. Mind you, Cullen would say that if all McMillan had done was steal a Mars bar.'

The superintendent's lips spread back a fraction across his teeth. He looked as if he was going to say something harsh, but it was only a warning. His mouth slackened again.

'Your attitude, Fletcher —'

'It's the result of twelve years' conditioning.' Fletcher glanced at his watch. 'I'd better get out and hunt for our villain.'

'Remember,' Foster said. 'Ring me.'

'Don't worry.'

Foster watched Mike walk to the swing doors, one hand in his baggy jacket pocket, the other pushing back his hair. They were both senior officers but they looked like they came from opposite ends of opposing scales. The fact was never lost on the superintendent. He let out an authoritarian sigh and moved to the dissecting table. The body, still tightly buttoned up, had been transferred to the scarred porcelain. Dr Garrett stood alongside. He was gowned, pulling on rubber gloves.

'Nasty business, Doctor.'

Garrett picked up a knife from the row along the edge of the table. He peered at it.

'It's never any different in here,' he said. 'One nasty business after another.' He pointed the tip of the knife at the body. 'When we get the clothes off we'll know a lot more, but I'd guess he died from a penetrating wound of the lung. The ribs are very creaky on the left side.'

The superintendent strove to look bewildered.

'The witnesses are saying he was booted fifteen or twenty times,' he said.

'So I gather. It takes a lot of anger to make somebody do that. Or a lot of fright.' Dr Garrett held out the knife to Albert Coker. 'Put an edge on that, will you? It's as blunt as my bum.' He turned to Foster again. 'I'm told you know who did this.'

'Steve McMillan,' Foster said. 'A right little bastard. Twenty-one last month, but he's got enough form for a villain twice his age. The way the story goes, Sergeant Lowther was having words with him outside a pub and McMillan jumped on him. Threw him down and started kicking. No warning.' Foster paused to reflect. 'An animal,' he announced.

'How's the widow taking it? I assume there's a widow?'

'Yes. They were separated. Somebody went round to see her. She was devastated, of course.'

Dr Garrett was being distracted by the body. He turned his back to Foster and pushed the dead man's head left and right, listening to the neck sounds. Albert Coker honed the knife quickly on an oiled stone and put it back on the table.

'Can't move for the press out there,' Foster said.

Garrett gave him a faraway look.

'Reporters. Crawling about the place like flies at a Pakistani wedding.'

The doctor made a tiny wince and Foster cleared his throat, a begrudged apology.

'I don't suppose there's anything we could tell them, Doctor?'

'You can tell them Sergeant Lowther's dead.' Dr Garrett nodded to Albert Coker, who started unbuttoning the dead man's tunic.

Foster cleared his throat again. 'I'll be at home, then. If anything important comes up, maybe you'll let me know.'

Dr Garrett mumbled something, helping Albert Coker with the tunic. Foster shook his head, lowered his responsible eyes, and left the dissection room.

THREE

Mike Fletcher stepped into the gloom of the Lamb and Bucket and counted the heads. There was no reason for that, or none he understood; it was something he did when he went into a pub without a plan of attack. He reckoned there were eighteen or nineteen people standing at the U-shaped bar. A further check, made on the three-yard crossing from the door to the curved end of the bar, confirmed there were no strange faces present. That was hardly a surprise. The Lamb was a pub strangers never tried. Its face was too drab, too much a part of the disheartening locale.

An old man sitting at the side looked up from his newspaper and nodded. Mike nodded back. He had no idea who the man was. He was often there, like a grizzled extension of the upholstery.

A mirror at the back showed Mike a shock image of himself as he stepped into the pool of light around the bar. He wondered if other people saw him like that. He always looked weary. Kate said he was a crumpled version of Richard Gere. He didn't know what Richard Gere looked like, but he was sure it couldn't be anything like that.

'Inspector,' the landlord said, duplicating the old man's nod. He didn't look pleased to see Mike. 'Working, are you?'

'Yes, Ralph, I'm working.' Mike put both hands on the bar, propping himself, thinking that although he didn't have a clue what Richard Gere looked like, he did remember Charles Laughton. The landlord was a dead ringer. 'I suppose you've heard what happened.'

People along both sides of the bar were observing, none of them directly. Each man present, Mike supposed, had something he didn't want a copper to know. It was that kind of place, a miscreants' boozer in a square mile of city where everybody practised villainy to some extent, or was at least tainted by contact with criminals. There were no barons of crime to be found here, no Mr Bigs or kingpins. The Lamb was for pedestrian crooks who shielded their credentials with expressionless faces.

'Yes, I heard.' Ralph shook his big head. 'Terrible news, Inspector. Terrible.' It was the thing to say and once it was said he moved on, abandoning the fabricated sorrow. His voice hardened. 'I can't believe what they're saying, mind you. About who did it. I can't believe that at all.'

'Steve McMillan did it. It's hard to believe, sure. But he did it.' Ralph's disbelief didn't budge.

'Doubt doesn't stand a chance,' Mike said. 'We've got too many witnesses. Sergeant Lowther was killed right out in the open, on a public thoroughfare in front of twenty-odd people. They all saw Steve McMillan putting the boot in. It's an open and shut job.'

The landlord's face was a wall of rejection, and Mike understood that. Tribal loyalty was cemented in unreasoning certainties. Confronting it was like challenging the dimwit piety of a Jehovah's Witness. No amount of reason, no logic, would uproot instincts nurtured on group prejudice and skin-deep fact.

'Even a good kid like Steve can kill somebody, Ralph. A hell of a lot of nice people commit acts of slaughter every day. It's a fact of life.'

'But Steve McMillan,' Ralph said. 'Him? A murderer?'

'I can't picture it. I'll admit that.'

'That's two of us, at least.' Ralph drew a damp towel along the bar. 'Are you having something to drink while you're here?'

'I'll have a Grouse. A large one.'

When Ralph brought the drink Mike asked if Steve McMillan's young brother had been in.

'Terry? Not tonight. He hasn't been around all week. He owes the slate, so I'll not see him till he gets his next Giro.'

Mike accepted that. He took a sip of his whisky.

'Have you pulled Steve in yet?'

'No. But we will.'

'Christ.' Ralph knuckled one eye and stared blearily across the room. 'I can't get to the bottom of it. If you lined up ten nuns and

Steve McMillan and asked me to point out the likely killer, I'd have to pick one of the nuns.'

Mike heard only part of that. He was distracted by the man who had elbowed open the door and was now sauntering over to the bar. Detective Sergeant Cullen walked with the same proprietary beat that governed his speech. This was a man who worked on his presence. He had the build of a rugby player running to fat and a facial belligerence that was entirely natural. He was thirty-five but looked nearer Mike's forty-three, with dark-ringed eyes and a drooping, thick-lipped mouth. Tonight he was slitting his eyes and his head had a fractional sideways tilt.

'Ernie,' he rumbled to the old man at the side, who nodded the way he had when Mike walked in. 'Keeping your nose clean, eh?' Cullen issued a grin, a cold one, maintaining his measured progress to the bar.

He had seen Mike the second he came in, but he wasn't looking at him yet. He was busy giving the rest of the clientele his special look, the slow-burning scan that said, *I'm a hard one, maybe the hardest.* When he drew up beside Mike he asked Ralph for half a pint of bitter.

'Any word?' he asked Mike, finally looking at him.

'Nothing yet, Percy.'

The sergeant's homely name was delivered loudly enough for the others to hear. Cullen's discomfort was the price for failing to acknowledge Mike's seniority when he spoke to him.

'Somebody'll find the lad soon, if they haven't already,' Mike added, swirling his drink.

'Maybe. I wouldn't put it past the shitbag to try and take off.'

'Well, yes,' Mike said, nodding. 'It must have occurred to him. I mean you'd consider it if this thing was hanging over your nut. So would I.' He gulped a fraction too much whisky and had to tighten his throat to keep from coughing. He looked at Cullen with watering eyes. 'The thing is, though, Steve McMillan hasn't got the nous to take off. He's not a worldly soul. Outside the home he doesn't have any relatives I know of, or many mates. His one overpowering urge, I'd imagine, is to get back home to his old mum. Right now he's hiding somewhere. But he can't do that for ever.'

Cullen stroked his nose slowly from bridge to tip. It was part of his image tool-kit, a gesture suggesting he submitted a thought to meticulous scrutiny before he gave it voice.

'I'll bet his brother knows where he is,' he said.

'That's who I came here to check on,' Mike confided. 'Like Steve, he's got a very limited range of haunts. He hasn't been in this one tonight.'

Mike knew Cullen would want to know where else Terry McMillan hung out. He also knew the big sergeant would sooner choke than ask.

'I haven't heard any theories yet,' Cullen said, trying for a ventriloquist's mouth and manoeuvring away from Ralph's ear-shot. 'Everybody knows what a Christ-awful thing it is that's happened, but that's all I've heard so far. I mean, I know McMillan killed Lowther, but nobody seems to have a notion what he did it for.'

Cullen waited for a theory while Mike emptied his glass and put it on the bar.

'It's the oddest thing I ever heard, Percy.' Mike buttoned his jacket, signalling his departure. 'I haven't even tried to speculate. I can't — there's no handle. Steve McMillan is one of the sweetest villains I ever met. What other burglar would stand shuffling his feet in the middle of the carpet when an old man catches him doing over his house? That happened last Christmas. He stood there blushing and apologising and waiting for us to answer the three-nines call. Came along like a lamb. He's always been a softie.'

'Until tonight,' Cullen said. He did a neck-stretch, easing his Adam's apple past the margin of his shirt collar. 'I hope I get first crack at the fucker.'

'I heard you'd been saying that.'

'I fancy I'm not the only one.'

'No, Percy, you won't be the only one. But maybe you're one of the few that means it.'

Mike said good-night to Ralph and left the pub. He walked the length of the street, turned left and peered into the dark. Four yards from the corner Detective Constable Chinnery flashed the lights of the CID car.

'Neat timing,' he said as Mike eased into the front passenger seat. 'I just got here.'

'Did you try the café?'

'Yes. And the arcade, the chippie and the disco. Nobody admits seeing Terry McMillan tonight. Nothing but dead ends, sir.'

'Think positively, Jim,' Mike winked at his fresh-faced young partner as he fumbled with the seat belt. 'Usually, if anybody wants to find Terry they find him. Fast. When he's not at home he's in one of his hang-outs. But tonight the men in funny helmets have been to see his mum and they're watching the house. He hasn't been there since early on. He hasn't been to any of the usual places either. Unheard of, that. Terry's missing, so he knows where his brother is.'

'That leaves us nowhere, doesn't it?'

'But we know a bit more. That's something, Jim.' Mike raised his left wrist and tilted it at the window, reading his watch by the street light. 'I think I might go and talk to Mrs McMillan. I meant to do it earlier but things got in the way.'

'DS Cullen's been round there already.'

'Shit,' Mike breathed. 'When?'

'About an hour ago, I suppose. I picked up his sidekick on the radio on my way back here. He was asking one of the lookouts if Terry had shown up since Sergeant Cullen had been to the McMillan house.'

'That settles it. I'll definitely talk to Mrs McMillan. Maybe I can undo some of the damage.'

'Do you reckon the DS leaned on her, sir?'

'Definitely. It's his best investigative technique.' Mike yawned. He was tired, but he knew if he got to bed before midnight he would only lie awake. Since Moira died he hadn't dared go to bed until he was exhausted. 'Cullen was in the pub just now,' he said, diverting his mind from a sudden picture of his daughter. 'He was doing his lethal-lawman bit. There'll be no holding him when his promotion comes through.'

For a silent moment they pictured the future.

'At least he'll be off this patch,' Jim Chinnery offered.

'He should be off the force.' Mike glanced at his partner. 'I know you wouldn't say it, but you know he thinks the same about me, don't you?'

'I know he doesn't like you, sir.'

'He hates me, Jim. I'll tell you about it some time. It's a story for a late-shift when we've less to do.'

FOUR

Kate Barbour sat cross-legged on the carpet, coiling strands of her hair round her fingers. Her other hand held the telephone a fraction of an inch from her ear. The voice from the earpiece was high and scratchy; as a reproduction of the real thing it was more accurate than a stranger would believe. Bridey Sloane was coming close to tears.

'It's unbearable,' she squeaked. 'I did everything you said, I tried to be calm and not fight it. I tried to distract myself. I even went out for a while, and you know how I don't like leaving the place at night. It didn't do me any good. As soon as I came back into the flat it was there, the awful smell. Stronger than before. So strong it makes my eyes water. I've been sick twice. I can't stand it.'

'Try to be calm, Bridey.'

She swallowed audibly.

'I keep worrying, too. About how I'll be if it goes on much longer. Does the condition send people mad? Or does it mean I'm mad already? Tell me, Doctor,' Bridey demanded. It was a rare burst of insistence. 'I'd rather know the truth.'

'Come on, now,' Kate said, 'what kind of talk is that? Your condition's nothing like that bad. I've no worries about your sanity. None at all.'

The lie was a necessary element of therapy. It also underlined Kate's position in the relationship. The psychiatrist, above all else, is the fountainhead of sympathy, and therefore the focus of hope. The fib soothed the patient and reinforced her belief in Kate's potency as a healer.

'If only other people could . . . could *take the measure* of this as well as you do,' Bridey sighed. 'They've no idea what I go through.

Not my husband, not my colleagues, not anybody. They've no idea at all.'

'It's difficult for other people,' Kate said. 'Yours isn't an easy condition to understand. Now tell me, how long has this bout lasted, would you say?'

'Four hours or so. I wasn't actually sick until about an hour ago. The second time was just before I rang you.'

'And do you feel sick now?'

'No,' Bridey said. 'Not so long as I hear your voice.'

'Could you identify the smell this time, Bridey?'

There was silence.

'Bridey?'

'I'm still here, Doctor. It's . . . it's difficult for me to say. To put a name to, I mean.'

'Then don't try, Bridey.'

Faeces, Kate decided. The only other patient she had known with the condition came right out and named it — 'Now and again there's this stifling pong of shit.' But he'd been a forthright little cab driver, batty as a moor-hen but uninhibited, whereas Bridey was a diffident, repressed librarian. If Kate had pushed her for a description of the imagined smell, Bridey would have gone into a lather, rummaging for a euphemism.

'It's indescribable,' she said, sounding tearful again.

'Just keep breathing steadily. That'll help you to relax. Don't feel threatened. Remember, anxiety makes matters worse.'

'Yes, yes. I know you're right, Doctor. I'm trying, I'm breathing like normal, like nothing's wrong.'

'And while you're doing that,' Kate said, 'try to imagine cool, fresh air blowing through the whole house, dissolving the bad smell and leaving every corner fresh. Can you do that?'

'Yes, yes . . .'

A time would come when the fresh-air method-acting ploy wouldn't work, when the air everywhere, even on the barest, windiest hillside would fill Bridey's nostrils with the stink of sulphur and worse. She was afflicted with a grimly realistic neurosis. It had the spiralling power to send weaker people mad, as Bridey had begun to suspect.

'Do you feel calmer now?'

'I think so.' Bridey sighed softly. 'Yes, I'm sure I do.'

They spoke for a few more minutes, until Bridey said she believed the attack had passed. The air in the house smelt clean. Kate told her to come into the clinic in a week's time, ten days earlier than their next scheduled appointment. Before Kate hung up she reminded Bridey to call whenever she wanted, and told her never to feel she was without support.

The phone was on the cradle less than ten seconds before it rang again.

'Hello? Kate Barbour here.'

'You're that young one with the red hair,' a man's voice said, throaty and muffled. 'You *are* her, aren't you?'

'What if I am?'

'Red hair, pouty little mouth, sexy figure, good legs. You're that one, right?'

'Who is this, please?'

'Guess what I've got in my hand, love.'

Kate frowned at the carpet.

'You can have more than one guess,' the man said.

Her frown cleared.

'Mike?' She heard laughter. 'You bastard!'

'I'm sorry.'

'What the hell do you think you're playing at?'

'It just came over me,' Mike Fletcher said.

'You should try to control yourself!'

'It took me five shots to get through, and you know what I'm like when I start getting bored.'

'Silly bugger. For a minute there I thought one of the clinic creepies had got hold of my number. Don't ever do that again.'

'OK,' he said, 'I'll try to behave more responsibly in future.'

'You're worse than a kid.'

'Absolutely right. I'll make every effort to grow up. How are you, anyway?'

'The same as I was last night. Can you remember last night?'

'Uhuh. In that case you're fine.'

'If a little shaken.'

'Listen, Kate, I wouldn't bother you this late, but it's business. Sort of.'

'Police business?'

'Afraid so. One of your patients is in trouble. I wondered if you could tell me something.'

'You mean,' Kate said haughtily, 'you want me to violate the confidentiality of the patient-doctor relationship?'

'That's right. Like you usually do when I ask you.'

'Who's the patient?' Kate asked.

'Steve McMillan.'

'What's he done?'

'He's killed a man.'

'Are you serious?'

'Completely. Earlier tonight he kicked a police sergeant to death. Does it sound unlikely to you?'

'It sounds impossible,' Kate said. 'Do you *know* Steve's the killer, or is he only a suspect?'

'He did it. Nothing's surer.'

'Christ . . .'

'You sound as surprised as I am. Do I take it you can't imagine Steve being a killer, even though you know a lot about his personality problems?'

'I'd say he couldn't do it.'

'Snap,' Mike sighed.

'So tell me more. Have you got him in custody?'

'Not yet. He took off. I've been to see his mum, she's in a hell of a state. She's got hold of the idea he might try to do away with himself.'

'It's not likely,' Kate said. 'But after what you've told me, who knows?'

'I think we'll find him before long.' Kate heard Mike yawn. 'I better go,' he said. 'I've been trying to get through to you so long, Chinnery'll think I've been kidnapped.'

'I'd a patient on the line,' Kate said. 'A magnet for nervous disorders. I was talking her down from an attack of cacosmia.'

'Sounds nasty.'

'It is.' Kate twiddled a strand of hair. 'I just can't believe this about Steve.'

'We'll talk about it tomorrow, my love. Wait till then.'

'If you say so.'

'And on that note,' Mike said, 'I'll get back on the job. Sleep tight, honey.'

'Good-night, Mike.'

Steve McMillan was on her mind as she got ready for bed. In her nightdress and flapping slippers she went round the small house checking locks and putting off lights. In the living room she stood for a minute with her hand on the light switch, staring at a framed *Saturday Evening Post* cover on the wall behind the couch. The illustration was a Norman Rockwell dated April 1946. Two cleaning ladies sat close together in the plush stalls of an empty theatre, reading a programme somebody had left behind. Kate loved the picture. The ladies, their expressions, the surroundings — the elements of the photograph added up to a warm portrayal of sane human order she found irresistible. For Mike Fletcher it added up to corny sentimentality. But Kate approved of controlled sentimentality. She had a tendency to stare at the picture when she was confused.

In bed, the mystery of Steve persisted, keeping her awake. She remembered he had missed two clinic appointments, so she hadn't seen him for a month. At their last meeting he had been jumpier than usual. More uncommunicative than usual. She had wondered then if he would try to drop out of the sessions, and hoped he wouldn't. Up to that point she had believed he was not a disturbed person, although he did need help.

Now, faced with the need to revise her evaluation, Kate couldn't. Nothing in Steve's character, as she had read it, would ever predispose him to violence.

She turned on her side and started retrieving Steve's case profile, piece by piece. Everything she could remember pointed to a man incapable of ordinary assertiveness. He was shy, unwilling to initiate friendships, mistrustful of change. His stunted personality operated from cover. He had no recreations beyond an interest in racing form. Steve was a mother's boy with counterfeit local colouring that caused him a lot of heartache. When he wasn't under the control of his mother he was influenced by other lads, most of them rough and into one sort of crime or another — and that gave Steve more problems because aggression wasn't in his makeup. He was deficient in the commodity, he actually *needed* some. If a man like that was left to be passive and dependent, then his instincts for ordinary survival would shrink and perhaps die. As matters stood, Steve had the makings of a social vegetable. How could he ever be a killer?

'Data shortfall,' Kate murmured as she closed the file in her head.

She was getting fidgety. Puzzlement had pulled her too far off the approach to sleep. She rolled on her other side, punched the pillow and shifted her attention to Bridey Sloane. Five minutes passed; she was wider awake than ever.

If she didn't sleep soon she would be useless in the morning. The general instructions for relaxing a patient were known to her, but they never worked when she tried them on herself. A colleague prescribed hot milk followed by reading a few pages of *Exchange & Mart*, on the principle that saturated fats calmed the nerves and the reading of one boring small-ad after another numbed the brain to the point of stupor. Kate was too careful about her weight and cholesterol levels to start taking regular milk drinks, and *Exchange & Mart* fascinated her. In early student days she had often made herself drowsy by mentally reciting a poem by Edward Thomas, *Lights Out*, that described perfectly the state of floating submission which precedes deep sleep. Now she couldn't even remember how it began.

She thought of Bridey Sloane again and admitted she wasn't much use to that lady. Or perhaps to anybody. She realised it was to be one of those nights, the kind when she was drawn to the insomniac notion that all she did was interfere in screwed up lives. On nights like this it was easy to believe she brought her patients no help, did nothing but delay ugly upshots that lurked on the far side of diagnosis.

Groaning, she rolled on her side again, resigned to stay wide awake until self-reproach stopped itching.

24

FIVE

'This has had it.'

Sidney Pearce held up the whisky bottle he had brought to Guy McKaskill's house. It had been full at ten o'clock. Now only a spoonful was left in the bottom.

'Funny how we abuse the stuff when we get it at supermarket prices. In the pub, I can nurse a double for an hour or more.'

From his armchair, McKaskill pointed to the sideboard, a heavy mahogany piece from the fifties with two dark, polished-over scars on one door where his son's tricycle had collided with it thirty years before.

'In there,' he said. 'Left side, top shelf. A half bottle of Crawford's I got off Derek last Christmas.'

Sidney showed a ferrety reluctance to get the bottle. He wrinkled his pointed nose and shook his head.

'I'm sure you'd sooner hang on to it, Guy.'

'If I wanted to do that I wouldn't tell you to fetch it, would I?'

'Whatever you say.'

Sidney got the whisky and brought it to the fireplace, where the dead bottle and empty glasses stood on a foldaway card table. He glanced at McKaskill, whose face was turned to the churning magi-coal.

'Will I open it, Guy, or would you like to do it? Any other time I'd not ask, but this being a special bottle, I thought maybe —'

'Just open the fucker and pour us a drink.' McKaskill glared at Sidney. 'You're like an old woman at times, know that? A pigging old woman.'

Sidney grasped the cap and gave it a half turn, snapping the seal. He unscrewed it quickly and poured two steep measures. He passed one to McKaskill, tasted his own, savoured it and threw back his head. His rubbery, deep-pouched face overdid his rapture grotesquely.

'Very nice, *very* nice. A lovely drop of stuff.'

McKaskill swallowed a mouthful of whisky. He closed his eyes as the liquid warmed its way to his stomach. His gaunt face was seraphic. The sharp, precise lines in the flesh were a theatrical complement to his cap of dense white hair. When he opened his eyes again, they fixed on Sidney. After fifteen years' acquaintance with McKaskill the little man still found it hard to look directly at those eyes. When they stared they demanded response, and Sidney knew that whatever was expected, it was even money he would miss the clue and say the wrong thing.

'Yes, yes, Guy,' he muttered, and cleared his throat. 'A very nice drop. It's not very often nowadays you get —'

'It's nearly midnight,' McKaskill said. 'I haven't been up this late for years.' He glanced at the door that led to the hallway and the stairs. 'Ella's been in bed since seven o'clock.'

'The shock, I suppose,' Sidney ventured, easing himself into the chair opposite McKaskill.

'She always goes to bed early. It's her arthritis. She only gets peace from it when she lies down.' McKaskill turned his face from one wall to the other, as if he might find something in the room to blame for his wife's condition. 'It beats me how she can sleep at all tonight, though.'

'I know I won't,' Sidney said.

They had talked for two hours. Sidney had exhausted his expressions of sorrow long before eleven o'clock, and as Guy McKaskill's remarks had grown fewer and shorter the little man filled the gaps with reminiscence and anecdote. Mostly he recalled the days when Derek McKaskill had moved among them, whole, a joy and a credit to his father. Now Sidney had run out of memories as well as condolences. He was tired and empty of things to say. He needed his bed. But he knew Guy McKaskill had summoned him here for more than company. Sidney would wait until he knew the score. Guy would tell him when to leave.

'I've been thinking, Sidney . . .'

McKaskill held his glass between both hands, lowering it out of sight between his knees as he looked slowly round the austere, fiercely tidy living room.

'At first it was all a jumble, you know? I was blazing mad, I was heartsore, I couldn't get my head straight. But sitting here, talking, letting things fall into place, I see it all clearer now. I'm sure about what's got to be done.'

His eyes had come to rest on Sidney again. Sidney swallowed some whisky. He hadn't a clue what to say.

'It's like doing a puzzle. You look at it and you see nothing but a mess. Confusion's all there is. But if you wait, keep looking and letting it all soak in, you see a shape. You see the sense of the thing.'

Sidney nodded, wondering what the boss was on about.

'The picture's very plain to me now.' McKaskill set his glass on the table and sat back. 'My son's paralysed. Nothing's going to change that. Yesterday he could walk. He's a big lad, a man, and he's always been able to look after himself. But . . .'

'Maybe it was like they said, Guy. He was picked on by mistake. That could be what it was, a terrible mistake.'

'Those fuckers tell you what they want you to hear,' McKaskill said sharply. 'What I'm saying is, my Derek is no nancy boy. He's hard, I brought him up that way. But in a place like that, in a nick where the balance of things is different, being hard's not enough. Half the long-termers inside are off their heads. I say this — if Derek hadn't gone in there, he'd be fit and well today. He'd have the use of his legs. Now that's it in a nutshell, right? That's the whole picture as it needs to be seen.'

'Definitely.'

'So somebody should be brought to book for what happened to Derek.'

Sidney gazed sadly at his drink.

'Getting at them,' he said, 'that's the hard bit, Guy. Getting at them. If they were on the outside it'd be a piece of piss, right? But they're not on the outside, are they? We'd have a hell of a job —'

'Will you let me say what I want to say?' McKaskill shouted, making Sidney jump. 'Just listen, for Jesus' sake. Somebody has to pay for Derek *being there*. That's what I'm saying. Do you get it? If my boy hadn't been put away, he wouldn't be in the state he's in now. So I want a job done on the shithouse that got him locked away.'

Sidney shifted his weight uneasily.

'The judge?' he said, dry-mouthed. 'Christ, Guy, that's a bit of a tall order.'

'No!' McKaskill roared. 'Not the judge! The cop, Sidney, the bastard cop!'

'Oh, him. Yeah . . .'

'It strikes me I should get a pencil and paper and draw you pictures from now on,' McKaskill said. 'You're getting so fucking dim there's no point talking to you.' He wiped his lips with the back of his hand. 'I want the cop. I want him hurt. Am I getting through to you?'

Sidney nodded, still agitated.

'Not easy, that,' he murmured.

'How come?'

'Nobody can just walk up to a cop, especially a senior one, and do the business on him. You know what they're like with their own kind. There was a cop got bumped off up in the city earlier tonight —'

'I heard,' McKaskill said. 'I took it as kind of a good omen.'

'The streets are crawling with uniforms. Arses are going to get kicked until they get the one they're after. They'll stop at nothing. That's how they take on when one of them gets done.'

McKaskill sat nodding for a while.

'So that's the way it is,' he sighed, picking up his glass again. 'You're not only a shit-brained old woman, Sidney. You've turned chicken as well.'

'Aw, come on, Guy, be fair.'

'Fair? Fair be fucked!'

Agitation drove Sidney to his feet. He crossed to the table in the centre of the room, used it as a turning point and walked back to the fireside.

'I think you should sleep on this idea, Guy. We've both had a few, haven't we? Maybe the thoughts aren't coming as straight as you think they are. A bit of daylight on the problem usually works wonders, right?'

Now McKaskill stood up. He towered a clear foot above Sidney.

'Are you telling me I'm too pissed to think clearly?'

'No, I'm not.' Sidney took a step back, so it would be easier to look up at McKaskill. 'You know I don't mean anything like that. But what *you're* saying isn't like you. You're careful, Guy, you've always been careful. That's the reason you've never been inside, it's the reason nobody's ever done you for anything.'

McKaskill turned away impatiently, facing the fire. Sidney risked closing the distance between them again.

'This idea about getting the detective,' he said, 'it's dangerous. The odds are the worst. And consider this, Guy — they'd connect you straight away. They'd see the link between what happened to young Derek and what happened to the bloke that put him away. They'd hound you. They wouldn't give you a minute's peace till they got you nailed.'

'Listen,' McKaskill growled without turning round. 'My mind's made up. I've explained that. It's the only explanation I'm going to give. And I don't want any arguments.'

'I was only making a point, Guy.'

McKaskill turned, fixing Sidney with cold eyes.

'You were in the court with me when the cop gave his evidence,' he said. 'Fletcher. DI Fletcher. Remember what he was like? Remember how keen he was, and the way he kept looking at our Derek as if he hated him? That wasn't just some bobby doing his job. It was personal.'

'Maybe,' Sidney conceded.

'If it hadn't been for the way that bastard delivered his story Derek would have pulled six months at the most. He'd have been out in two or three. Christ, for all we know he might have got off with a heavy fine. But no. Oh, no. Mr Big Stick wanted the judge to hand out a three-stretch and the arsehole got what he wanted.' McKaskill inhaled and let it out unsteadily. 'It's my turn now. I know what I want and I'm going to get it.'

Sidney shrugged. Capitulation to the will of Guy McKaskill was inevitable, whatever the misgivings.

'How do you want to do it?' he asked.

'I need to know where he'll be at a certain time.'

Sidney didn't hide his surprise.

'You're talking about doing the job yourself?' he said. 'Is that what you're saying?'

McKaskill nodded.

'But you don't want to take a risk like that, Guy! Christ, there's no need! Nobody keeps dogs and barks himself!'

'This job is mine,' McKaskill said, sitting down.

'But if —'

'Just shut up, Sidney.' McKaskill spoke softly, which was worse than having him shout at you. 'Get me a time and a place — some place remote enough and reliable. If you've any trouble tracing Fletcher's movements, speak to Martin Reynolds.'

Sidney curled his lip at the mention of the barrister's name.

'That beauty. It gives me the pukes just thinking about him. I mean it's one thing to be a bent lawyer, but a *bent* bent lawyer — that's something else.'

'I don't like him any better than you do,' McKaskill said. 'But he knows the cops. He's in with them, he knows their habits and their movements. That big poofter is useful, so we'll use him.'

McKaskill swallowed the rest of his whisky in one gulp and put the glass down. Sidney caught the dismissal. He finished his own drink and said he had to go.

'Give this priority,' McKaskill told him. 'I want to hear from you soon.'

'I'm on it already,' Sidney promised. He went to the door. 'Good-night, Guy. Give Ella my commiserations, won't you?'

'I will,' McKaskill nodded. 'I'm sure it'll be a comfort. Just you see I get the chance to have mine.' He folded his arms and stared at the toes of his carpet slippers. 'An eye for an eye, Sidney.' He looked up. 'That's fair enough, isn't it?'

SIX

Steve listened to the clock bell in the distance — it would be the one on the church two streets from where he lived — and he counted twelve.

He must have been in the old prefab for hours. He hadn't stood up since he scrambled in through the broken window and threw himself into the corner. There was no feeling in his feet and his back hurt so bad he knew he would have to straighten it soon or something would give way.

The fear assaulted him in waves now. He would have whole stretches when all he felt was miserable and tired, wondering what he was going to do, where he could go. Then the terror would come sluicing down on him, a panic that shivered through his bowels when he realised all over again how bad it was, how black and terrible. Jesus God, it was the worst. It was the *very* worst. What was burglary or theft or even GBH compared to this? Safety was gone, hope blacked out. They would get him and when they got him it would be too horrible to think about. He would be shut away, maybe for the rest of his life. Unless he found somewhere to go, some place to run. But he didn't want to run . . .

There was someone outside. He knew it, *felt* it like a shift in the air. His breath stopped while he listened. *Yes, Christ yes!* Somebody was outside, walking carefully, sliding along the wall near the window. Steve crouched. He put his hands over the back of his head and pulled his face close against his knees.

Please God, don't let them get me!

The sound of movement got quieter, more distant. Whoever it was, he was moving away, off to the left. Maybe just a prowler, some tramp looking for a place to put his head. That would be it. Steve looked up as the door grated open.

'Steve?'

Relief gushed in him, so powerful it brought on the tears again. He scrambled to his knees and crawled to the door, whimpering.

'It's all right, Steve, it's me.'

He reached up and grabbed his brother round the waist, hugging him, crying against his jacket.

'There now, take it easy.' Young Terry, cocksure by habit, took his brother under the arms and lifted him. 'Come on, over here and sit down, eh? I brought you some grub.'

Steve let himself be led back to the corner. He sat on the bundled rugs and lino, pulling his windcheater about him.

'Got enough here to feed an army,' Terry said, unslinging a plastic carrier-bag from his shoulder. He started unpacking takeaway containers, setting them in a row in front of Steve. The first and second fingers of his right hand were missing. He used the hand like a claw around the tinfoil boxes. 'It's all Chinese, the stuff you like. Special fried rice, sweet-and-sour pork, beef and ginger — you owe me a packet.'

'I don't want anything,' Steve said.

'You've got to eat.'

'Sod eating! I don't want it!'

Terry stopped unpacking the carrier, pushed the boxes aside. He came and knelt beside Steve. In the dim light his young face looked older.

'What are you going to do?' he said.

Steve was motionless for a while, transfixed on a dark picture of his future. Then his shoulders started to shake and he was out of control, sobbing against clenched teeth.

'Somebody should tell them,' Terry said. 'They ought to know about that Lowther.'

Steve struggled to pull himself under control. He put his head back and inhaled shakily.

'How'd you find me, Terry?'

'It didn't take a lot of guessing. You're always talking about this place, all the fun you had here when you were a kid. Not long ago you told me it would make a great hideout for anybody that needed one. Remember?'

Was that it? Steve wondered. Was that why he came running straight here? This place did take up his mind a lot. He even dreamed about it. Maybe it meant so much because those days had been the best. Things had got worse since. There wasn't the fun any more, none of the laughs.

'You better not come back here,' he said to Terry. 'They'll follow you.'

'Nah. Not a chance.'

Terry was sharp tonight. This was front league stuff, he was the only person in the whole city who knew where his fugitive brother was hiding. Concerned as he was, Terry was on an elongated buzz.

'What about the old lady?' Steve said.

'I haven't been back to see her yet. I thought the coppers would be hanging about.'

Steve remembered Terry had been a witness. He hadn't been more than five yards away when it happened. There was a flashing vision of Terry frozen, staring as the policeman rolled over, clutching his chest.

'Some bleeding mess, Terry . . .'

'You've got to hold on to yourself. Keep remembering it's OK here. Nobody knows this place, just me and you.' Terry leaned close and squeezed Steve's arm. 'We'll get something worked out.'

Steve unwound the crucifix from his knuckles, rewound the chain until it was taut across the backs of his fingers.

'He made me do it.'

'I know that,' Terry said.

'Who'll believe that? Who'll want to? You know what coppers are like.'

Terry edged closer and put both arms round his brother's shoulders.

'We'll get it sorted some way,' he whispered. 'You'll see.'

SEVEN

The body of Sergeant Lowther had first been opened from throat to pubis. The organs of the chest and abdomen had been cut out one by one, examined, cut in slices and examined again. Specimens were taken for lab examination, then the organs were dropped, piece by piece, back into the cavity of the body.

Next, the scalp was divided across the top from ear to ear and folded over at front and back to expose the cap of the skull, which was then sawn off with an electric plaster saw. The brain was taken out, sliced thinly and examined under a powerful light; samples were put in labelled bottles. The remaining slices were placed in the abdomen with the other chopped organs. To give weight to the emptied skull cavity, a couple of soaked sheets of newspaper were wrapped around the kidneys and shaped to fit the brain pan; the damp mass was then pushed into position. The top of the skull was replaced and the scalp stitched with twine. When Mike Fletcher arrived at the mortuary a few minutes before one in the morning, Albert Coker was finishing the closure of the abdomen with an S-shaped needle and the same rough twine he had used to close the scalp. Dr Garrett was by the dissection-room door, whistling softly as he took off his plastic apron.

'I was beginning to think you'd crossed out my name in your social diary,' he said as Mike stuck his head round the edge of the door. 'Caught our murderer yet, have you?'

'Not yet. I don't think we will, tonight. We'll get him some time in the next twenty-four hours, I imagine.'

'Have you time for a quick one?'

'I thought you'd never ask.'

The doctor pulled on his jacket and straightened his tie.

'Thanks for hanging on, Albert,' he said to the attendant. 'Your mini-cab will be along in about twenty minutes.'

Albert Coker looked up from the body, nodded and murmured something inaudible. Dr Garrett and Mike went along the corridor and into the office. The only light in the room came from an anglepoise lamp on the desk. Mike sat down. He watched the old pathologist unlock the deep bottom drawer and pull out a bottle of Glenmorangie. He poured two measures into miniature lab beakers and passed one to Mike.

'Confusion to the enemies of the Queen,' he said, raising his glass, swirling the whisky once, then downing half of it in a single smooth swallow. 'Lord, that's better.' He dropped into his swivel chair, slumping for comfort. 'You've come to talk about the case, I suppose.'

'Not especially.' Mike tasted his drink. 'I wanted to chat. It's been a couple of weeks since we talked. The last time I saw the light on and looked in, Dr Brodie was here.'

'Preparing to don the mantle,' Garrett said. 'Don't misunderstand me, Mike. I like John Brodie, but he could make his impatience less obvious. I've four years to go.'

'I'll miss you. We've put the world to rights in this office a lot of times, over the years.'

'Indeed. A fair quantity of malt's flowed through the hepatic duct.'

'Enough to drown a camel.'

They were silent for a moment, friends together, content with each other's company.

'This isn't a night I'd have expected a visit,' Garrett said. 'I was listening to your führer earlier, demanding utmost speed.'

'Archibald Foster's henlike panic breaks out every time he thinks the press might level a personal criticism at him. It happened once, years and years back. As criticisms go it was pretty oblique and nobody but Archibald noticed it. This case has got an extra dimension for him, of course. He's dead keen to get spotlighted as the lightning-fast cop who collared a cop killer.'

'He'll take the credit, you fancy?'

'Sure he will.' Mike rubbed the stubble on his chin. 'Let's not talk about him. He's a disheartening topic for this time of night.'

Garrett nodded and took up the bottle again, uncapping it. He topped up Mike's glass and his own.

'I'm sorry you don't want to talk about the case,' he said. 'It's an odd one.'

'So we'll talk about the case.'

Garrett put the bottle back in the drawer and sat forward, bracing his elbows on the arms of the chair and lacing his fingers on the promontory of his stomach.

'I know about all kinds of violence, or the results of it. In the context of my experience, this case is nearly unique.'

'How?'

'The assailant kicked a rib right into his victim's heart. That's unusual, even if your attacker's on the heavy side. My report will describe the degree of force as extreme. Maniacal would be a better word. Demonic would be better still.'

'I know the kid who did it,' Mike said.

'A tearaway, according to your superintendent.'

'Not at all. He's a bewildered, maladjusted, chicken-hearted boy. Got a pretty fair build, but he'd be no good at throwing it about.'

'That's intriguing,' Garrett said. 'But tell me, do you know much about the dead man?'

'He was a loner. No social life, no outside interests. Spent his nights-off at home, or in the police club playing dominoes with his inspector.'

'He lived for his job, do you think?'

'Definitely.'

'God, the ironies that crop up in this place.' Dr Garrett leaned further forward. 'I'll tell you this now, but it won't become official until later. Sergeant Lowther wouldn't have stood a chance of passing his next police medical.'

'How come?'

'Before the broken rib shut that heart down for good, it had started to die anyway. Lowther was suffering from advanced heart failure.'

'Christ.'

36

'I was in touch with his family doctor less than an hour ago. The sergeant saw him three times in the past two months. He was warned his heart was in poor shape.'

'He knew all about it?'

'Oh, yes,' Dr Garrett said. 'He'd been suffering from dyspnoea — shortness of breath — at night, and sometimes during the day. He told the doctor it had been going on for near enough a year.'

'What was the cause?'

'His blood pressure was very high. That meant the blood from his lungs wouldn't be pumped adequately by the left ventricle. It would begin to accumulate in the pulmonary circulation. The lungs would get congested, and that would make Sergeant Lowther wake, desperately breathless, in the night, frightened, staggered by his mortality. Heart failure's a cumulative business. To put the block on it he would have had to live a very quiet life. In short, he needed to retire.'

'What about the assault?' Mike said. 'Would a man with a normal heart stand up better to something like that?'

'No. Death was due to a traumatic rupture of the right ventricular septum. A hole like that would kill anybody.'

Mike took out a packet of Rothmans and lit one. The smoke spread out around him like winter mist, backlit by the beam from the lamp.

'It's some picture,' he said. 'We have a boy who's never raised a finger against anyone in his life, who attacks and kills a man who shouldn't have been on his feet at that time of night, much less pounding a beat.'

'Yes. It's an odd one.'

Mike's look had regressed to melancholy fatigue.

'It's at times like this I feel like chucking it,' he said.

'Starved of light relief? You've talked about getting out before. I suspect the thing that made you join is the same thing that keeps you from leaving.'

'What would that be?'

'Concern.'

'Maybe.' Mike said it dismissively. 'What brings on the gloom with this case is an old problem of mine. I've always felt more than

37

naturally edgy about cases that throw up suspicions of . . .' He shrugged. 'Sticky human darkness, I suppose. There's a hell of a lot more to this than meets the eye, isn't there?'

'I'd imagine so. But your concern, Mike — it's still there, surely?'

'Maybe,' Mike said again.

'Mine is,' Garrett sighed. 'It's what's kept me in daily contact with all the sadness and horror that turns up in this charnel house.' He yawned. 'I believe I'm getting drunk. Another one before you go?'

Mike shook his head. He stood up and drained his glass.

'Duty,' he said.

'You're going to carry on working?'

'Well . . .'

'You're going to carry on for as long as it takes to get you exhausted.' Dr Garrett pulled himself to his feet. He slapped Mike's shoulder. 'It'll get better,' he said.

'I don't know if I want it to. My nightly agonies are an act of proper remembrance, I suppose.'

'For the time being. But that perspective will change, too.' Dr Garrett opened the office door. 'There's no charge for the prognostication. Good-night Mike.'

A squad car was drawing up in front of the mortuary as Mike came out. The passenger door opened and Superintendent Foster stepped out, dressed in civvies now. He stood looking at the CID car, then twitched round to face Mike as he came down the steps.

'I thought you were at home, sir,' Mike said, making it casual.

'And I thought you were out looking for McMillan.'

Mike sniffed, as if the superintendent's petulance had a smell.

'He's hiding. But we'll find him, I don't think there's any worry about that.'

Foster went through an overdone mime of impatience. He rolled his eyes and tutted. Mike watched dispassionately.

'When felons hide, Fletcher, that's when we're supposed to work hardest. We're obliged to unearth them. What in hell are you doing here?'

Mike stepped close.

'I'd take it kindly,' he said, 'if you wouldn't address me like a wet-arsed recruit, especially when your driver's listening in.'

Foster did his speechless-with-affront routine. Mike stared at him, willing every trace of submissiveness out of his own nature. Foster's insecurity began to flash. Even his body was a giveaway. He straightened his neck, squared his shoulders, tried for an imperious angle of the head.

'I asked you a question,' he said.

'I've enough rank to operate on personal initiative,' Mike told him. 'I was visiting the mortuary for what I judged to be sound reasons.'

'You haven't communicated with me once since we spoke in the mortuary. DS Cullen has phoned in *twice* to report progress.'

'Oh, he's made progress, has he?'

'For God's sake!' Foster yelped. 'I've got Regional HQ leaning on me, the press . . .'

He checked himself and glanced back at his driver, who had his window down and was looking interested.

'The press,' Foster continued, quietly now, 'a TV crew with a very pushy interviewer . . .'

'Tell them we're not chasing a crazed killer. That'll damp down the panic. Let them know we're after a scared kid, and say we'll find him soon.'

Foster leaned forward sharply, his nose nearly touching Mike's mouth.

'Have you been drinking?' he demanded.

'What's that got to do with anything?'

'Just answer my —'

'Jesus! Yes, I've had a drink.'

'Marvellous!' Foster looked around as if there was some crowd on hand to witness this discovery. 'Absolutely bloody marvellous!'

Mike swung on one foot, putting himself squarely in front of Foster.

'What is it with you? You squeal like a bandicoot every time you get me in your sights.'

'You're a hooligan, Fletcher! A disgrace!'

39

The weariness edged off Mike's face. His jaw stiffened. Foster inhaled shakily and dropped his voice again.

'No discipline. No respect. You always have to run the show your way. Eight weeks I've put up with it and I'm not taking any more. Plain clothes and a bit of rank doesn't give you the right to flout the rules or tramp all over authority. Do I make myself clear?'

'Put the bellyaches in your report,' Mike said. 'And quote me on this — I don't find it palatable or in any way necessary to jump through hoops for a uniform man who's only standing in for my DCS. *Please* quote me.'

He turned away, pulling out the car keys. He could feel the superintendent's shape on the pavement behind him, a shaky monolith. Bed, he decided, striding to the car. Bed, and the swift bludgeon of sleep. He was suddenly tired enough.

EIGHT

Martin Reynolds knew that late nights and early mornings were the times when he was least in control of himself. He believed that each new day his personality assembled itself in stages, then disintegrated again, piece by piece, as the evening wore into night. When he woke up in the morning, scarcely more than the animal was there. As the first waking hours passed he swore he could feel the civilising layers swathing him one by one — reason, mature judgement, caution. Only then did he show himself to the world, a handsome, smooth-groomed, sharp-witted man of the law, a barrister of cunning and intelligence who could manipulate the law with a touch so light it seemed debonair.

It was eight in the morning, so Martin felt distinctly basic. No caution yet, no judgement. He propped himself on one elbow and looked at the sleeping boy in the bed beside him. The hair was dark and soft-curled, the face unlined and finely contoured, girlish except for the hardness at the mouth. Definitely under age, Martin decided.

He strained to remember the night before. Nothing came. Alcohol, sadly, could punch out whole stretches of his memory. His mouth tasted bad and his head thrummed, so he'd probably had a bucket last night, washed out the last traces of caution and picked up this sweetie in one of the awful places they haunted, the dank little drinking clubs with stony-faced doormen and zombie barmaids. Another pickup, another frantic session between the sheets. Another one he couldn't remember.

Reason would tell Martin he had taken a terrible risk. Some of these cherubic little bastards were lethal — he had prosecuted a case where a man was hacked to death in his own house, mutilated beyond recognition by a rent boy with the looks of a Botticelli angel. Others, too many, simply liked to beat men up. There were blackmailers among them, too, and theft was epidemic. The most honest, non-violent lad could harbour AIDS. But these reflections would come and worry him later. For the moment Martin was his fundamental self, without the refinements, growing tumescent as his hand crept out over the boy's leg and cupped the heavy genitals.

The doorbell rang. The boy opened his eyes. Martin froze, looking at the clock. Who in hell could it be at this hour? Christ, not Dermot, surely not yet, he wasn't due back for hours . . . No, not Dermot, definitely not, he had his keys, was never without them. Martin decided to stay where he was. If it was important the caller would come back.

'What time is it?' the boy asked.

'Early. No need to rush.'

'Was that the door?'

'Yes. But I'm not in.' Martin slid closer, his hand working. 'I never see visitors before breakfast. And before breakfast I like to put in some exercise. It gives me an appetite.'

'Yeah, me too.'

The doorbell rang again. They looked at each other and Martin cursed under his breath. The bell rang again. This time the caller leaned on it for ten seconds before he let go.

'Shit!'

Martin rolled out of bed and grabbed his dressing gown. He slipped it on, belted it, and told the boy to stay put. On his way along the hall he paused at the mirror and patted his silver hair into place at the sides. His skin looked rumpled but there was nothing he could do about that. He moistened his lips and teeth, as he did in court before he delivered one of his fine-tuned torrents of abuse. The bell rang again. Martin stamped to the door and jerked it open. There was a weasely little man on the step.

'Sorry to bother you so early,' he said.

'I'm sorry you did, too. That bellpush isn't a musical instrument, you know. Nor is it a fire alarm.'

'I didn't get your attention the first time or two. Can I come in and have a word?'

'No, I don't think you can.'

'Disturbing something, am I?'

The baiting was clear, but Martin never rose to anything like that.

'Who are you, exactly?' The face was familiar, but the context was too vague to pinpoint so early in the day. 'What do you want?'

'My name's Pearce, Sidney Pearce. I'm an associate of Guy McKaskill. It was Mr McKaskill that asked me to come and see you.'

The penny dropped. Martin had seen this character hovering around McKaskill and had assumed, no doubt correctly, that he was just another seedy henchman.

'Why couldn't he come himself? And why does it have to be at such an ungodly hour?'

'Mr McKaskill's a bit busy just at present,' Pearce said, narrowing his small eyes. 'I came round early because I didn't want to run the risk of missing you.'

'So tell me what you want. It's freezing out here.'

'It would be easier if we went inside.'

Martin didn't want this charmless little fart in his house, especially in the present circumstances. But it really was cold and in nothing but a dressing gown he would run the risk of a chill if they didn't go inside. He held the door wide and waved Pearce into the sitting room. Following him in, Martin was sharply aware that his books, his precious porcelain figures, his Chinese carpet and Castrofilippo furniture did not deserve the violating presence of such a scruffy, lowlife, soiled-looking man.

'Nice place,' Pearce said, nodding at a bentwood table, a couch, a reproduction Praxiteles wrestler. 'Very nice.'

'So. Explain your errand.'

Pearce's face hardened. Even this tawdry shambler, Martin thought, could show ferocity behind the eyes. It was a jungle-dweller's reflex — when they were barked at, the impulse was to bite.

'I'm not an errand boy, Mr Reynolds. I'm an associate of Mr McKaskill, like I told you. You might say I'm his right-hand man.'

'It's not a thing I'd be likely to say. But fine, fine. You've told me all I need to know about your status. Now can you tell me what you want?'

'Some information,' Pearce said. 'You're kind of friendly with a policeman —'

'What policeman?'

'Detective Inspector Fletcher.'

'I doubt he'd agree that we're friends. I have a certain regard for the man, it's true, and my work brings me into contact with him.' Hearing his own bitchy edge, Martin registered a new observation: when he was annoyed by a certain type of person, he sounded like a piping old queen. 'What does McKaskill want to know about Mike Fletcher?'

'His movements, as a matter of fact.'

'What?'

'Places he goes when he's off duty. As a habit, that is. Regularly, you know? Especially places he goes on his tod.'

'What makes you think I'd know anything like that?'

The words were a mask for a thought process. Martin sized up Pearce's mission swiftly.

'If I'm not mistaken,' he said, before the little man could answer the question, 'McKaskill's son was put away on Mike Fletcher's evidence. That fact makes me recoil from your request, Mr Pearce.'

'Eh?'

'What are you up to?' Martin demanded.

Pearce made a one-sided grin and spread his hands, a spider insisting he was a ladybird.

'Look, you know this man, you've done the prosecution on a lot of cases he's brought to the courts, and people have seen you having drinks with him. I've clocked the pair of you myself a couple of times. We're just asking you, as somebody that's acquainted with Fletcher, to give us some idea about his movements. Our reasons are nothing to you.'

'Go back,' Martin said, 'and tell Guy McKaskill I can't help him.'

'Now that's unreasonable,' Pearce said, putting in a guttural hint of menace. A warning finger came up. 'Mr McKaskill isn't going to like it if I tell him you don't want to co-operate.'

'Listen to me, my shitty little friend.' Martin stepped close to Pearce, showing him a strong jaw and the determined eyes of a courtroom carnivore. 'It's a matter of supreme indifference to me what McKaskill is or isn't going to like. There is no way I'm going to abet some murky scheme to visit mischief on a man I happen to admire — a man, I might say, who has done no more than his duty where McKaskill's son or any other criminal is concerned.'

Pearce spent a couple of seconds looking indecisive. Faced with Martin's unrelenting bulk, he finally decided to go back to the door. Martin followed him.

'I think you'll be sorry about this,' Pearce muttered, going out to the hall. 'Guy McKaskill isn't a man that likes being turned down.'

'You'll notice I'm wilting with fear.' Martin jerked open the front door. 'Kindly don't come here again.'

Out on the step Pearce raised his finger again.

'Guy's going to —'

'For all I care,' Martin interrupted, 'he can take a flying fuck at a rolling doughnut. Please go.'

Pearce went. Martin slammed the door. He pounded back to the bedroom on his bare feet, hands buried in the pockets of his dressing gown. The boy was out of bed, standing naked by the window. He turned to face Martin and stretched slowly, smirking.

'I think you should get dressed and go.'

The boy frowned.

'I thought you —'

'Just piss off,' Martin snapped.

He left the bedroom and went to the kitchen. The cafetière was on a shelf with the percolator and the teapot. He took it down and pulled too hard on the plunger. It jammed. He cursed and gave it a jerk. It came free suddenly. His hand flew back, hit the grinder and knocked it over. Coffee beans showered across the floor.

'Damn it to hell!'

He looked down at his feet, making himself breathe slowly. The civilising layers would be slow in coming today, he thought. All because of a visit from a shoddy little nothing. Because of the threat he represented. Martin wondered how long it would be before McKaskill turned up in person, bringing his gutter menace with him, his danger.

He kicked at the spilt beans and reminded himself that the sheerest strength is in the mind, which fires the will. They could throw all the threats at him they liked, he would still have no part in their plans for Mike Fletcher. He knew he could work up the determination to stand by that. Until McKaskill showed up, of course. At that time, depending on the magnitude of the threat, all bets might be off.

NINE

Mrs McMillan came to the door the third time Mike knocked. She was dabbing a crushed paper tissue to her nose. Her eyes were red and she looked weary.

'Sorry to bother you again, love. Can I come in?'

She stepped back. Mike went in, waited until she closed the door, and followed her into the living room.

'Nice and warm in here,' he said, nodding at the mobile gas heater in the middle of the floor. 'How are you feeling?'

She sat on the end of the creaky couch, saying nothing. Mike looked round the room. It was a pastiche of post-war furniture, Boots prints, and what was once called the Wonder of Woolies. The Boy With a Tear was framed on one wall and above the boarded-over fireplace was Tretchikoff's Eurasian lady with the blue face.

'No word from young Terry yet?'

Mrs McMillan shook her head, still dabbing with the tissue.

'And I suppose you still haven't been able to think of any place Steve might go on his own, if he wanted to get away from things?'

'I don't know none of the places he goes, him nor Terry for that matter.'

Mike nodded. His call was more social work than policing, anyway.

'Have you been to bed?'

'I slept for a couple of hours on here.'

'You should have gone to bed. You look all in. If you don't get proper sleep you'll make yourself ill.'

She *was* ill. There was a copy of a health visitor's report back at the station: in 1977 Mrs McMillan had been cured of TB, but

47

scarred lungs, poor nourishment, years of worry and hardship had left her spiritless and frail, vulnerable to every germ and virus that touched her. Recently anaemia had crept into the picture and the family GP believed she showed signs of incipient diabetes. She reminded Mike of his grandmother in the last year of her life. Mrs McMillan was twenty-three years younger than Grannie Fletcher had been when she passed away.

Mike sat down on the other end of the couch.

'Don't let the worry get on top of you,' he said.

'Can't help but worry.'

'I know. But try not to let it wear you down.' Mike clasped his hands on his knee. 'I wish we could find Terry, you know. I'm sure he could take us to Steve.'

'That Cullen said I was to ring him the minute Terry came back.'

'I'd rather you rang me, love.'

'Yeah, so you said last night.' Mrs Mcmillan looked around her and the tears started up. 'Everything's so quiet . . .'

'Will I make you a cup of tea?'

She thought about it.

'That'd be nice.'

Mike went to the kitchen and lit the gas. He filled the whistling kettle and while he waited he looked out of the window. He could see the car across the road. Chinnery was slumped down behind the wheel with his collar turned up. There was no sign of Cullen's car, but he wouldn't be far away. Misery drew him on when it could fire his indignation, his urge to punish.

Mike turned to the sink and ran warm water into the teapot, swirled it and tipped it down the drain. Spooning in the tea-leaves, he remembered Cullen once admitting, in the squad room, that classic murder cases had him in thrall. He was an enthusiast, he could recite the minutest details, the oddest pieces of investigative detail about murders committed more than a hundred years ago. It had emerged that he was intrigued by self-appointed executioners of felons and degenerates, and in cases where such killers had never been identified his fascination amounted to obsession.

When Mike brought the tea to Mrs McMillan she took the mug with both hands. He sat down beside her again, noticing how the mug shook when she raised it to her mouth.

'I'm not here to scare you or threaten you, love. I want to make it easy for Steve, or as easy as I can. Now do you believe that?'

She blew on the tea.

'That Cullen,' she said, 'he told me they'd crucify Steve.'

'That's rubbish.'

'I could tell he meant it. And he said he'd see to it we get a hard time if Steve don't show up today.'

'Most of the time,' Mike said, 'Detective Sergeant Cullen blows through a hole in his neck. You leave everything to me. I won't let anybody hurt Steve.'

Mrs McMillan's false teeth clicked as she swallowed her tea.

'What could've got into him, our Steve? He's not as much as hit anybody before . . .'

'Best thing is you leave it,' Mike said firmly. 'The fretting gets you nowhere and it makes you feel worse.' He looked at his watch and stood up. 'Promise me, as soon as ever Terry puts in an appearance, you'll go out to that phone box and ring the number I gave you. If I'm not there they'll pass the message to me on the radio and I'll be round straight away. And remember, love, tell Terry it's best to talk to me as soon as possible. There's no use him trying to stay out of sight, he can't do that for ever. OK?'

Mrs McMillan nodded, blinking at tears again.

'Them two's all I've got,' she said. 'I keep thinking that.'

'Ssh.' Mike touched the bony angle of her shoulder. 'Drink up your tea.'

Back in the car he looked at his watch again and tutted.

'Nearly eleven o'clock. I thought we'd at least have had Terry by now. Anything on the blower?'

'Nothing, sir,' Chinnery said, 'apart from a bulletin about more mobiles being brought in at noon if we still haven't found Steve McMillan.'

'That's Foster playing nerve games with the troops. Psyching them up. Nobody wants outsiders getting the medals.' Mike looked up and down the empty road. 'Tell you what. I'm going to

49

hoof it for a while. You stay here in the nice draughty car and keep an eye out. Terry might be daft enough to come back to the house the front way.' He undid his seat belt. 'You know what he looks like, don't you?'

'Sure,' Chinnery nodded. 'Short-arsed tearaway. He's got a mop of bleached hair, pimples, bandy legs, and there's two fingers missing off his right hand.'

'That's him,' Mike said. 'It could have been worse than two fingers, if he'd been slower off the mark.'

'What happened?'

'Five years ago. Terry was only twelve or so. He tried to screw Gupta's fish and chip shop. Old Gupta caught him in the back room and went for him with the gutting knife. The surgeon's report described Terry's stumps as a defensive wound.'

'Bloody hell — the Indian chopped his fingers off?'

'It's a fact. The kid had his hand over his goolies when it happened. That's where Gupta was slashing about with the knife.'

'Was there much of a case?'

'If Mrs McMillan had had the savvy and the cash to get a decent brief, there would have been. As it was, Terry got off with a caution and a modified mitt. Mr Gupta was fined and warned about the future consequences of applying Eastern methods of justice in a Western society.' Mike pushed open the door and stepped out on to the pavement. 'I'll catch up with you later. Don't forget to signal me if anything develops.'

He slammed the door shut, waved to Chinnery and walked away along the road.

Half a mile to the south Terry McMillan was sliding in through the door of the rusty prefab where his brother had been hiding for fourteen hours.

'Steve? You still there?'

In daylight it didn't look like the same place. The drama had vanished. It was a filthy dump, bleak and disheartening. Terry wrinkled his nose at the smell.

'Steve?'

In the corner by the window the bundle of stiff brown-black

carpet moved. Steve put out his head. His face was dirty and tear-streaked.

'You all right?' Terry came forward and put a lumpy parcel on the floor. 'I brought you an anorak. A scarf and a balaclava, too.'

'Where'd you get them?'

'Ask no questions, I'll tell no porkies.' Terry tried to grin. 'I've some sandwiches in my pocket. You've got to be hungry by now.'

Steve crawled out of his stiff tent and stood up. He looked miserable.

'I could do with something to eat,' he conceded. 'How's Mum?'

'I haven't seen her yet. Been busy. But I'll go round to the house today some time.'

'Do it as soon as you can. She'll be scared.'

'Sure.'

Terry went to the broken window and looked out. He came back, slapping his arms on his sides.

'It's cold as a witch's tit in here. One more night of this and you'll get pneumonia — if you don't catch something off all the crap on the floor before then. I've got a better place for you.' He took out a packet of cheese-and-pickle sandwiches and handed them to his brother. Steve tore open the wrapper and bit the corners off both sandwiches at once. 'It's warm and it's as safe as this gaff,' Terry said. 'Safer, even.'

'Where?'

'Machin's. The brewery. It's just a warehouse now. There's only the old guy that looks after it, nobody else goes near. All he does is fire up the boiler to keep the place dry.'

'He'd find me.'

'Nah. The hideaway I know, it's right at the top of the building. Nice clean little room, it's even got a bog outside the door. I can get you a sleeping bag, a primus, all the necessaries. If you wanted, you could hang out there until all this blows over.'

'It's not going to blow over.'

'They can't keep looking for you for ever. You could get away after a while. Lose yourself somewhere. Happens all the time.'

'How come you're so sure the old guy there wouldn't find me?'

'Because he's really *old*. It's all he can do to get the fires stoked and sit on his arse until his shift's finished. Anyway . . .' Terry winked knowingly; 'I don't reckon him or anybody else knows about the room any more. It's up two flights, through a trap door and up another flight with bales of paper and old chemical drums blocking the way. Perfect hideout, Steve. Honest.'

'But you know about it. If you know, other people know.'

'Nah. I found it nearly a month ago, all on my own. I was in there looking for anything worth lifting. There's fuck all, but at least I found the room.'

'Is there a window?'

'One,' Terry nodded.

'High up the wall, or could I look out of it?'

'It's just like a house window. You can see for miles from up there.'

Steve stood motionless, a part of the wretchedness of the derelict house. He chewed slowly, thinking. Height and distance would make him an onlooker, somebody separate. That was the way he felt safest.

'Sounds better than this,' he said.

TEN

'There's been too much delay already,' Superintendent Foster said, tapping his pen on the window ledge. He stared at the sheen of rain on the glass. 'I want that bastard brought in before another day goes past.' He turned to Detective Sergeant Cullen. 'I'm relying on you, Percy.'

'Yes, sir.' Cullen heightened an inch. 'I can't help thinking I'd have had him by now . . .'

'But for the obstructions.' Foster's lips pursed. 'I'm not unaware of the problem.'

'Well, it's not for me to point the finger, sir . . .'

'It isn't simply that a certain other officer hasn't been pulling his weight, which he never does anyway. He's also been unpicking the fabric of this hunt, if we can call it a hunt. It's not the first time he's done it.'

The men looked at each other, righteous faced, cementing their complicity.

'I put the frighteners on Mrs McMillan,' Cullen said, 'but he's been round there, patting her hand and telling her not to worry. That's as good as telling her to stay shtoom. And I think he knows places where the kid brother might show up, but he won't share the information.'

'And he won't phone in.' Foster contemplated the arrow-shaped clip of his Parker Rollerball. 'He wants to get to McMillan first, just so he can get in a bit of psychology before the process of law takes over.'

'And we all know where he gets his encouragement for that kind of thing,' Cullen said, smirking discreetly.

'I've known policemen to slip it some odd places,' Foster said, 'but up a psychiatrist's a new one on me.'

'He'd be better off in Social Services, sir.'

'True enough. I can just imagine him campaigning for darkies' rights, or trying to reunite molesters with their children.'

Foster shook his head, gazing round his austere office. It looked as if a minimalist had been put in charge of the design, stripping the place with flair, leaving nothing on the beige walls but a couple of pictures as clues to the occupant's calibre: in one he smiled grimly beside a celebrated prosecutor on the steps of the High Court, in the other he was on the range in earmuffs and baseball cap, holding up a trophy for marksmanship. A framed citation on the filing cabinet, dated October 1980, declared that Chief Inspector Archibald Foster had shown extraordinary valour during a raid on a covert IRA cell in the city. The desk had a spotless blotter, a gilt-and-onyx combination penholder, letter-rack and calendar, a telephone and a picture of Mrs Foster. The swivel chair behind the desk was covered in grey tweedy material and the one in front was plain wood, straight-backed. A patterned rug was the only extravagance. It looked out of place.

'I'll have words,' Foster said. 'Higher up. Things'll get straightened out.'

'Very good, sir.'

'Meantime get back to it. Find Steve McMillan and drag him straight to the cells. I want him talking. I want him charged before tea-time.' Foster went behind the desk. He put down his pen and squared his shoulders at Cullen. 'This is no ordinary case, remember. This animal murdered a police officer. When our own are touched we have to react with vigour.'

'Definitely, sir.'

'Right now it looks to the press and the public like we're running round in half-arsed circles getting nowhere. That's bad for our image. For our morale. Very bad.'

'I quite agree,' Cullen said, creasing his forehead.

'So just you get out there, Percy, winkle out the thug and nail him. Try to ignore the obstructions — a certain person might not be around much longer, if I get my way.'

Cullen nodded and left, smiling tightly. Foster sat down behind his desk. The telephone rang.

'Foster here.'

The Chief Constable spoke at him in sharp bursts.

'Yes, sir,' Foster muttered. 'I'm confident we'll bring him in before long . . .'

Three more bursts.

'Yes, yes sir, you'll be the first to know . . .'

The line went dead.

Foster put down the receiver. His hand dropped to his crotch and scratched absently. How much rank did he need, he wondered, before he could wake up in the morning feeling safe?

Cullen found DC Bourton alone at a table in the canteen, smoking. The thin-faced young man had been a detective for less than a year, but he was used to senior officers keeping him waiting.

'You can buy me a coffee, Peter. A jam doughnut too, if they've got any that were made this month.'

Cullen sat at a table near the window and stared out at the rain. When Bourton came back with the coffee and doughnut Cullen pointed to the chair opposite.

'A small briefing,' he said. 'Bear with me a minute while I top up my sugar levels.' He took two wide-mouthed bites from the doughnut and slopped coffee in after them to soften the wad. He chewed for a minute and swallowed with a soft gulp. 'That's better.' He brushed sugar from the sides of his mouth and narrowed his eyes at young Bourton. 'I don't suppose you got anywhere?'

'I tried a dozen places, Sarge. Nobody's seen Terry McMillan today.'

'He's like a fucking ferret. We should have slowed him down long ago. It's what they did on a lot of the city forces, before the civil rights prawns started interfering.'

'Did what, guv?'

'Cut fast movers' speed as a matter of policy. You know what I mean — a broken foot going down the steps to the cells, a well-aimed truncheon round the knees on a dark night. Something lasting.'

'A bit barbaric, isn't it?'

'Fire's the best remedy for fire,' Cullen snapped. 'Gentleness should be reserved for handling valuable things. Villains are the dross of our society, son. Worthless shit. Having a few of them with their gearshifts busted was no bad thing.'

'I suppose not,' Bourton said, appalled.

'When anybody needed to know the kind of stuff toe-rags like Terry McMillan always know, they didn't have any trouble catching them. When my old DI wanted information, he used to tell me to go and ask one of the crab people.' Cullen laughed. 'Crab people, that's what he called them.'

He attacked the doughnut again. Bourton tried not to watch. He stared at the rain making sparky V shapes on the roofs of the cars in the yard.

'Right, then.' Cullen tipped the coffee cup to his mouth, emptied it noisily and set it aside. 'This is your programme for the rest of the day — keep out of my way. End of briefing.'

Bourton stared at him.

'Are you kidding?'

'I kid with my equals, Peter.'

'But I thought we had orders —'

'*We* don't receive orders.' Cullen jabbed his own chest. '*I* get orders. I interpret them. When I've done that, *you* take orders from *me*.'

'What should I do, then? I mean, I'm on till seven.'

'Go to the pictures. Go twice. Or hang about the Nanking Takeaway and make the Chinks nervous. Do whatever you want, so long as you don't come anywhere near me. If you accidentally see me anywhere, fuck off in the opposite direction.'

'Whatever you say, Sarge.'

'Oh, and if you're asked at a later date how you spent your time today, you'll say you were with me. On a seeking-out tour of the city and outskirts.'

'Fair enough.' Bourton took out his cigarettes.

'You can go now,' Cullen told him. 'Blow your smoke in somebody else's face.'

★

Mike Fletcher accepted a paper cupful of coffee from Kate Barbour. She put another coin in the machine and filled a cup for herself.

'Follow me, lawman.'

She led the way along the corridor. They sat on a bench outside the psychiatric clinic.

'Coppers are good at this,' Mike said, tasting his coffee. 'You know — turning up at the right time for a share of whatever's going.'

Kate crossed her legs, making her white coat rustle.

'Any word on Steve McMillan?' she asked.

'He's still at large. Or at small, more likely. He'll be in some pokey hidey-hole somewhere, sucking his thumb.'

'The papers are full of the murder. I thought about it for a while last night.'

'You didn't come up with anything that might help us, did you?'

'Nothing. It still doesn't make sense.' Kate started to drink, then stopped. 'I nearly forgot. Did you hear about Derek McKaskill?'

'I heard,' Mike nodded. 'Crippled. Assailant unknown, but the governor thinks it was a mistake.'

'A *mistake*?'

'Not the attack, the target.'

'He was kicked down two flights of stairs. Poor devil.'

'That was my first reaction,' Mike said. 'Poor bloke, what a terrible thing to happen — then I thought about the nightwatchman, Mr Purdie. Remember him? Consider what happened to *that* poor man, anchor your perspective on those facts. When you do that it's easy to believe nothing's too terrible for Derek McKaskill.'

'But you wouldn't wish this kind of thing on him, would you?'

'No. But I can't think of any suitable punishment. To suffer the way he made the nightwatchman suffer, he would need to have that old man's humanity. And he hasn't.'

'It was a ghastly case.'

'Foul. He carried on torturing Purdie long after he'd got the keys and all the information he wanted. He tore out a chunk of the man's hair and half scalped him in the process. He broke both his wrists and burned him with a cigar —'

'I saw the report,' Kate said.

'And you saw McKaskill.'

'I'm not likely to forget.'

At the time of the trial the court had appointed Kate to make a psychiatric evaluation of McKaskill. Mike had been the arresting officer. It was the first time he and Kate had met.

'A sociopath, you called him,' Mike said. 'I kept meaning to ask — is that the same as a psychopath?'

'Same thing. Nowadays a lot of psychiatrists prefer to say the patient's got "an antisocial personality", rather than hang a one-word label on him.'

'But all the descriptions mean the same. He's a vicious nutter.'

'The Victorians would have called him a moral defective. He's got no feelings of guilt, no natural human warmth. Sociopaths lie, cheat, exploit other people. They can't tolerate advice or criticism. It's not a disorder of thought or mood, it's a disorder of character.'

'There are lots of liars and cheats and exploiters. What makes the sociopath different?'

'Complete indifference to other people's feelings.'

'Derek McKaskill to a tee,' Mike said. 'I never wanted to see somebody get put away as badly as I did with that one. I think I turned into a full-weight crusading cop for a while.'

'It was a bad time for you,' Kate reminded him. 'Moira had just died.'

'I took my bitterness out on McKaskill, can't deny that. But he deserved everthing he got. More than he got. He should have been stuck in Broadmoor for the rest of his natural.'

'He won't do much harm now.'

'Don't count on it. What's the betting he goes in for a bit of hit-and-run with his wheelchair?'

Kate's bleeper sounded. She sighed and switched it off.

'For the wicked, no peace.' She stood up. 'Sorry, Mike.'

'It's OK. I have to go anyway. I really only called in to say I might be late tonight. But I *will* be round.'

'I'll keep a light in the window.'

'Dearest heart.'

Mike backed away, puckering his lips, making what Kate called his Tweetie-Pie mouth. An old woman going past stared at him. Kate went into the clinic, giggling.

ELEVEN

Guy McKaskill put out his hand and squeezed his son's wrist. Derek jerked his arm away.

'Steady, steady,' Guy soothed.

'Keep your paws to yourself, Dad. I don't need patting like some kid.'

Dressings covered Derek's head and most of his face. Thick pads covered both eyes. At the margins of bandage and lint Guy could see livid discoloration on the skin. He looked away, gazed along the ward. There were four other patients. Even if the uniformed guard hadn't been standing there at the door, anybody would know this was a prison hospital. It was on the men's faces, the vapid shut-away look, the despair.

'Anybody else near us?' Derek murmured.

'Eh?'

'Can anybody listen in?'

'No.' Guy looked behind him. The nearest man was three beds away. 'No chance, son. What is it?'

'I know who did this.'

'How come?'

'I was lying here listening. Sod-all else I could do. Just lying, making out I was sleeping. I heard the screw talking to a doctor. Dimmock's the one, he said. He wasn't where he should have been when I got done. They grilled him and he said he'd been playing cards in the recreation room. A load of bollocks, but they couldn't pin this on him.'

'Have you got a beef with this Dimmock?'

'None. I hardly know him. The screw reckoned he was after Laurie Edwards. Got confused in the dark, went the wrong way on

59

the landing.' Derek took a long deep breath. 'He'll be well fucking confused when I've finished him. He'll be lying here with his windpipe up his arse.'

'How will you get to him? You can't walk, and you'll not be going back to a cell anyway. As soon as you're fit to be moved, you'll be out.'

'I'll still get him,' Derek said. 'I'm owed. I'll put in a deputy.'

His father wanted to touch his hand again. He wanted to hold him, squeeze him the way he'd done when he was a baby. To see him like this tore at Guy's heart.

'How's the pain, son?'

'I told you, my back and my legs are dead. I don't feel anything. I've got a sore head and face, that's all.'

For a moment Derek tensed and Guy wondered what it was. Maybe he had glimpsed his future, whiffed years of misery.

'I'm going to do some fixing myself, Derek.'

'What's that supposed to mean?'

'The bastard that put you here, in this prison. I'm going to get him. I came here to make you that promise. It won't change anything for you, but it'll be a bit of justice. You might get some peace knowing that.'

Derek was quiet for a minute.

'Fletcher? Is it him you're on about?'

'Fletcher,' Guy said.

'You're off your head.'

'Maybe. Maybe not.'

'No maybes. The cops'll fucking roast you.'

'Ssh.' Guy looked up and down the ward. He leaned closer to Derek. 'Did you ever know them put a finger on me? Even once? No. Never. Never me, Derek. Even when they wanted to and tried, they couldn't. And this time isn't going to be any different.'

'Cobblers. You never went after a cop before — that'll make this time different.'

Guy could have wished for more understanding, a hint of appreciation and respect. But the boy wasn't himself. He was hurt and he was bitter.

'Stand on me, Derek. The thing's got to be done, and I'm the man to do it.'

'Yeah. Well.' Derek shifted his head carefully on the pillow. 'I think I want to have a sleep now.'

'Sure,' Guy said, 'you do that.' He had gone husky at the sight of the poor lad, his big strong Derek, brought to this. 'Got to save your strength, son. Get all the sleep you can.'

When he was outside the gates he looked at the sweep of the city's northern rim, a mile away. He saw rows and clusters of buildings, big and little, some new, some time-blackened, others falling down. Houses, factories, warehouses. There were scribbles of smoke in the sky and the sounds of bustling traffic. Once he had loved all that, the agglomeration that enticed with its opportunities and scampering possibilities, its cover, its promise. Now it seemed flat and no longer various. He had heart and drive for one thing only, one act to cool his scalding hurt.

'Are you ready then, sir?' the minicab driver asked him.

'Sure, I'm ready,' Guy said, getting into the car.

TWELVE

On a bench seat by the side of a greasy canal, Mike Fletcher sat with his coat collar turned up around his face and his hands buried in his pockets. He watched a man a hundred yards away throw a shapeless bundle into the water and wondered if he had witnessed the final stage of a grisly crime, or just another citizen adding his measure to the pollution of the defunct waterway. Whichever, Mike wasn't about to take any action. He'd done nothing ten minutes before when a woman allowed her dog to foul the narrow towpath, or before that when a tall schoolboy and a woman with orange hair picked their way out of the bushes and went off in opposite directions. Down here a man could get diverted from his purpose if he acted on every breach of the by-laws, or challenged suspicious behaviour. Mike kept his eyes on the brick hut by the road bridge and tried to ignore the cold.

Five minutes after the mysterious bundle finally sank, he saw the shed door move a fraction. He stared and it moved again. There was no wind blowing, so unless a small creature had nosed its way in, the door was being opened by some person crouching behind the cluster of willow herb half obscuring the entrance to the shed.

Mike rose and walked slowly toward the bridge, keeping well back from the canal edge. He stopped a yard from the shed, listened, stepped forward and jerked open the door. Terry McMillan spun, startled. He was holding a sack.

'Know something?' Mike said. 'This is the first hundred-to-one shot that's ever come up for me.'

Terry licked his lips and glanced past Mike.

'No chance, Terry. If you try it, I'll drop you before you're half-way out.'

'I wasn't doing anything.' Terry let the sack fall to the floor. 'Honest. I was just having a look round.'

'What were you doing that for? You know this place inside out.' Mike stepped in and pulled the door shut. 'You've been in here so often, I bet there's an old law somewhere that says you own the place by now.'

He looked around the dusty interior. He could understand why Terry used this place to stash his gear and bring girls when he got lucky. It was off the highway, and in spite of being so close to the canal it was dry. With a stove and a quick clean-up it could be made cosy.

'Do you remember who I am, Terry?'

'You're police. A detective. I don't know your name.'

'Detective Inspector Fletcher. We've met a time or two. Never socially.' Mike put his hands in his pockets, leaned close to Terry. 'So where's your brother?'

'No idea.'

'Aw, Terry . . .'

'He took off, after what happened.'

'And so did you. You haven't been home. Your Mum's worried sick. Where have you been since last night?'

'I was with a mate. Stayed at his place.'

'What's his name?'

'I don't remember. I only met him last night.'

'And you're not sure where he lives, because it's somewhere up on the new estate and you're not familiar with the layout.'

'Well yeah —'

'Terry, do you think my head zips up the back?'

'I'm telling you the truth.'

Mike took his hands from his pockets and slowly folded his arms. He leaned on the door post, staring at the boy.

'I can't blame you for protecting Steve. But let me put you in the picture —'

'I told you, I don't know —'

'Listen. I want to help Steve. What's going to happen to him when he's caught isn't going to be easy for him, but I can make it easier than it might be. Can you believe that?'

Terry drew his chin close to his neck, the body language of rejection.

'Maybe you'll find it easier,' Mike said, 'if I tell you this — I *know* Steve wouldn't have done what he did unless something was badly wrong. He's not a fighter, he wouldn't hurt a fly. I *know* that, Terry, and I can only think somebody was putting terrible pressure on him.'

'Fucking right,' Terry blurted.

'Tell me about it, then. I do want to help, and I might be the only one.'

Terry looked out of the little window for a minute. Mike waited.

'I don't know,' Terry said at last. 'I don't want to go making things worse for Steve.'

'They can't get worse. With a bit of luck they might get better. Tell me about it, Terry. Was it Sergeant Lowther? Did he have something on Steve, or what?'

'He'd nothing on him.'

Three short, agitated steps took Terry the length of the shed. He turned and came back.

'I'm not sure I should —'

'Let me have it,' Mike said. 'Without waffle or bullshit.'

'It went on for weeks,' Terry said, staring at the window. 'I told Steve, he should've got on to somebody about it.'

'About what?'

'It was that thing at Bremner's . . .'

'The cash-and-carry?'

'Yeah. A geezer done it over, five or six weeks ago. No idea who it was. Steve got a whisper it was some spade, a Brummie.'

'Steve wasn't involved?'

'Nah. He was nowhere near. And that's straight. But that Lowther, he got on to Steve the next week and said he would pinch him for it.'

'No evidence?' Mike said. 'Be sure, now.'

'I told you, didn't I? But Lowther kept on and on. Told Steve he'd do him, no matter what. Went looking for him, just to tell him that.'

'Why do you think he did that?'

64

'Well. Lowther was anti, know what I mean? When Steve got off the breaking and entering at Marks' last Christmas, Lowther took it personal. So like I said, when the Bremner's thing came up, he started putting the arm on Steve.'

Mike stood away from the door jamb.

'Are you telling me that Sergeant Lowther wound up in the mortuary because he was leaning on Steve?'

'No, it wasn't like that —'

'That's the way you told it.'

Terry was shaking his head.

'It was more. It wasn't — it wasn't just *leaning*. It got like cruelty. Lowther would turn up places where Steve was — he even used to ring him at the pub. It got so Steve was looking out for him all the time.'

'Were you there when any of this happened?'

'A couple of times,' Terry said. 'We were in the Lion one night, me and Steve. Lowther sidles up, all neat in his civvies, smiling like he's an old mate. He starts to go on about what a time it's taking to clear up the Bremner's job. "But it'll be straightened out soon, won't it?" he says to Steve. Then he says he's heard Steve applied for a job at Melford's. Steve tells him, yeah, that's right. "You won't get it, son," Lowther says. Then he pisses off.'

'Did he do that, stop Steve from getting the job?'

Terry held up three fingers of his good hand.

'Three jobs. The manager at one place was really keen to take Steve on, but he said they couldn't go through with it, what with the law being involved.'

'Did Steve tell you what else was going on?'

'Some of the time. Week before last it got real heavy. Steve was getting edgy anyhow, and Lowther starts ploughing in about maybe hanging a rape on him.'

Mike stared at him.

'A rape?'

'That's right. He said he could find ways to pin it on Steve, and then he starts telling Steve what they do to young blokes in prison, especially if they're in on a sex charge.'

'How did Steve take all that?'

'He was a nervous wreck,' Terry said. 'He shut himself in his bedroom a lot. A couple of times I heard him crying. And he smashed his aeroplane — it was a model he made. Loved it, he did. But this one night, he smashed it to bits.'

'Had he ever done anything like that before? Broken things, I mean?'

'Never. He's not like that. He always made me look after belongings when I was little. Anything at all. Steve treasures things.'

'And all this time,' Mike said, 'he wouldn't report what was happening to him?'

'No way. He said it would only make things worse.' Terry looked directly at Mike. 'He was really scared, you know. All the threats, they started piling up on him. I never saw anybody that frightened before. Last night, I had to talk him into going out for a drink.'

They looked at each other.

'Christ.' Terry looked at his bunched hands.

'It's not something to dwell on,' Mike said. 'What happened might have happened any time.' He put a hand on Terry's shoulder. 'Why don't you tell me where Steve is? I've got no grudge. Other coppers might have.'

'Even if I knew . . .' Terry looked around, everywhere but at Mike. 'I couldn't shop my own brother, could I?'

'Not even if it would save him a bit of grief?'

'I don't know that, do I?'

Mike looked hard at Terry and decided he wouldn't talk. Not yet. Things had to soak in, he had to weigh the situation for himself. Till then, no information, and maybe not even then. This was a tough cookie.

'What's in the sack?' Mike said.

'Just stuff I was going to move, I doss here now and again, it piles up . . .'

Mike lifted the sack and looked inside. There was a spirit stove, a thermos flask and three cans of soup. He put down the sack.

'Here's the position, Terry. If I take you in for questioning, other people are going to get at you. None of them are pussycats like me. One or two are bears. Maybe you don't think they can make you talk, but some of them certainly can, and you won't like the way they get you to do it.'

Terry's chin went in against his neck again.

'I don't care what you say, I don't know anything and —'

'Shut up and listen. I'm saying you better be good at staying out of sight.'

Terry frowned.

'I can go?'

'You can go. Nobody'll try to tail you. But if another policeman catches you — and there's a lot of them on the lookout, mind — I won't be able to help. You'll get the rough treatment, hours of it if necessary, and you'll wind up doing Steve no favours. Have you got that?'

'Yeah.' Terry was getting back his cocky look. 'When I work at it, nobody can find me.'

'Then you weren't working at it today. *I* found you. You'll have to try a lot harder.'

Terry nodded.

'And promise me,' Mike said, 'on your mother's life, if you're in a position to tell where Steve is, and you can make yourself understand it'll be a good thing to pass on the information, you'll get in touch with me and only me.'

'Yeah. Promise,' Terry mumbled, shuffling. 'On the old lady's life.'

'Right.' Mike pulled open the door. 'I'll bugger off. Watch your step.'

THIRTEEN

By one o'clock Singleton's Grill was filling up. In amber-lit alcoves, on stools along the plush-fronted length of the main bar, professionals and business people foregathered to initiate or clinch deals, to swap intelligence and reinforce their separateness from the rest of struggling humanity. Singleton's, with its hush-inducing carpet, its costly fittings and murderous prices, was the domain of high-power hustlers and conspicuous achievers. At the bar, immaculate in a dark-blue pinstripe suit, a scarlet carnation pinned to his lapel, Martin Reynolds exhaled the first puff of his second cigar of the day.

'Sophistry, dear,' he said, addressing Dermot Calder, the suntanned young man on the stool next to his. 'It's the whole basis of my style, and I suppose it's what's made me.'

Out of the blue, Dermot had asked Martin how he had come by his formidable success. They had known each other for eighteen months, and for half that time Dermot had lived in Martin's house; even so it was only now, fresh from a holiday in Greece, that Dermot showed curiosity about his lover's professional eminence. The week before, in the bar of a hotel in Athens, he had heard one Englishman tell another that if he really wanted to hammer his ex-wife in a lawsuit, he should retain Martin Reynolds. The other man said he had heard a lot about Reynolds, and he supposed he would be cripplingly expensive. The best always is, his friend reminded him. The exchange had made Dermot realise that he shared his life with something of a celebrity. If there was one phenomenon that fascinated Dermot more than any other, it was celebrity. He had always adored the idea of being famous. Fame by association was an acceptable substitute.

'What's sophistry?' he asked.

'Some people would say it's just faulty argument, but that doesn't do any justice to the art. What I do, what I'm *best* at, is finding ingenious ways to make clients' leaky cases sound absolutely watertight.'

'How?'

'Oh, I use tricky syllogisms, circular reasoning, well-timed barefaced lies, all sorts. It depends on the case. I'm also rather good at blowing holes in my opponents' attempts at sophistry, which is a useful weapon.'

Dermot frowned, watching Martin's cigar smoke spiral past the lampshade above the bar. To understand anything he had to receive it piecemeal. Too much information in one lump confused him. He didn't want to ask what syllogisms were, he was sure the explanation would only bog him down.

'So you're sort of a good actor, is that it?'

'That too,' Martin said. 'But acting's the embellishment, the dressing. The art's something else, it's an instinct at the core of me.'

Dermot nodded, still frowning a little. Martin flicked his ash into a silver ashtray on the bar.

'Tell me, Dermot, why so curious all of a sudden? I expected to be regaled with stories of your wonderful holiday. I thought you'd be breathless to tell me. Instead of that you come at me with questions about what makes me tick.'

'The holiday wasn't much,' Dermot said, dodging the question. 'I was missing you after the first day.'

'You shouldn't have been so impulsive, then. I told you, if you'd waited one more month I'd have been able to delegate some of my case load and come with you.'

'I'll listen to you next time,' Dermot promised. He turned his face fully to Martin, his blue eyes wide. 'I hope you behaved while I was away.'

'Of course I did,' Martin lied smoothly. 'I've had an extraordinarily chaste couple of weeks. No need to ask if you've been a good boy, I suppose.'

'No need at all,' Dermot said.

69

Which of course was true. His loyalty was a burden to Martin. Beautiful, personable, a gifted stage dancer with a modestly promising future, Dermot's only serious shortcoming was that he lacked a sense of adventure. He knew none of the glee of regular, illicit pursuit, the excitement of unpredictable outcomes, the warm guilt of certain stored secrets. As Martin saw it, he and Dermot would make ideal conspirators, lovers who could none-the-less freelance and share their delectable secrets. But Dermot was as faithful as a good wife and he expected nothing less of Martin. If it weren't for the fact that Dermot spent two weekends of every month in Dorset with his parents, Martin would have found the situation intolerable.

'I believe that man's looking at you,' Dermot said.

'What man?'

'By the door. The tall one with creepy X-ray eyes.'

Martin looked. Dermot saw his face stiffen.

'You know him?'

'I'm afraid so.'

He hadn't expected McKaskill to show up so soon. And certainly not here. He was coming across, his eyes fixed on Martin.

'Maybe you should leave us, Dermot.'

'Something private?'

'Don't be petulant. It's just that —'

Martin cut off sharply as Guy McKaskill came into earshot. He stopped by the two men, flicking a glance at Dermot.

'Why, Mr McKaskill . . .' Martin turned from the bar, propping his elbow. 'I don't believe I've seen you in here before.'

'No, you haven't.'

Martin introduced Dermot. McKaskill nodded without looking at him again.

'I suppose you know what brings me here, Mr Reynolds.'

Martin strove to look puzzled.

'You told my associate, Mr Pearce, that you didn't want to co-operate with me in a matter he explained to you. That's right, isn't it?'

Martin nodded. The genial look had gone.

'Maybe you didn't get the point,' McKaskill said. 'It wasn't a request.'

'What was it, then?'

'A transaction. I wanted to spend some of my credit.'

'I don't think I understand that.'

'Like fuck you don't.'

McKaskill's growl was feral. Dermot looked from one man to the other. The lightning shift from informal exchange to raw menace shocked him.

'I don't think this is the place —' Martin began, but McKaskill silenced him with a jab on the breastbone.

'Twenty-four hours. That's what you've got. I want a time and a place where I can be on my own with you-know-who. No witnesses. And no fucking tip-offs, if you know what's good for you.'

McKaskill spoke so quietly no one but Martin and Dermot heard, but the stance and expression loudhailed his malevolence. People were watching.

'I don't have to take this,' Martin hissed.

'Yes you do.' McKaskill buttoned his jacket. 'If you try to block me on this, I'll sink you. For good.' He stepped back a pace. 'Tomorrow, your place, one o'clock. I'll be round.'

He turned and walked away. The other customers stopped being a crowd of onlookers and broke up into murmuring groups. Dermot stared at Martin, who looked shaken.

'Who *is* he?'

'A bad man,' Martin said. He took a gulp of his highball. 'Somebody I should never have dealt with.'

'What is he?' Dermot was radiating protective concern. 'He seems to have a hell of a grip on you.'

Martin swung round and put his elbows on the bar. Dermot did the same.

'Guy McKaskill is a criminal,' Martin said. 'No speciality, he's a general practitioner. Not high-profile, not low-profile. He's no-profile. A Teflon man. Nothing sticks. He's into larceny, coercion, vice, drugs. And blackmail, of course.'

'How did you get mixed up with him?'

71

'An error of judgement, I suppose. I was prosecuting a case, eight years ago, thereabouts. He approached me and offered to hand over documentary evidence that was very damning to the defendant. It was just the thing I needed. I didn't like the look of McKaskill, but I was in a corner. So I accepted and I won the case. It didn't hurt my career any. Then a couple of months later he was back, asking me to defend one of his people on a robbery charge. I explained I didn't handle that kind of case. "You do now," he told me.'

'You couldn't refuse?'

'No. By then he had something on me. An indiscretion, set up by McKaskill himself, as it turned out. The boy was under age and he was prepared to lay a complaint.'

'Oh.'

'Since then McKaskill has felt free to retain me whenever one of his friends or associates needs a good barrister. I get my fee only when I win a case.' Martin shook his head at the bar. 'Thank God I was out of the country when his son's trial came up. McKaskill would have turned very vindictive if I'd lost that one — and I would have lost it.'

Dermot gazed along the line of bottles behind the bar.

'Your mistake was attracting his attention in the first place,' he said.

Martin nodded slowly.

'Astute of you, Dermot. If I'd turned down his bloody evidence in the first instance, I'd have lost the case and he'd have lost interest in me. But he was on the lookout for a good trial lawyer at the time. What he calls a class brief. And when he was sure he had found his man he got the dirt on me. It's how he works — if he needs somebody, he makes sure they can never refuse him.'

Dermot ordered fresh drinks.

'So what was that all about just now? It didn't sound like anything to do with a trial.'

'No, it wasn't.'

Martin explained what McKaskill wanted.

'This morning I had a feeling it had something to do with his son's imprisonment. What I've learned since then confirms it.

72

Young McKaskill's been worked over by another prisoner. He's in a bad way and Daddy's out for blood.'

'This policeman he's after, Fletcher — you've talked about him once or twice. Isn't he the one you call — what is it?'

'The Archangel,' Martin said, smiling faintly. 'Much to his discomfiture.'

'What's behind the nickname?'

'Good God, it's not a nickname.' Martin sat up from the bar and tasted his drink. 'It's a title, Dermot. His name is Michael and in the Christian faith the Archangel Michael is the chief opponent of Satan and his angels. In the Koran he's an Archangel too — Michael, the champion of the faith. Very appropriate. And there's the other Archangel, the port on the White Sea in the Soviet Union — a cold, relentless place, a metaphor for Fletcher in his vengeful mode. I can say with a straight face that Mike Fletcher has a purity and directness of purpose that's unusual in a policeman. It can rise above the messy inadequacies of the law, if it has to. He denies all this, of course.'

Dermot twirled his glass.

'What are you going to tell McKaskill when he comes back? Can't you say there's no way you can get the information he wants?'

'He knows different,' Martin said. 'Policemen, especially senior detectives, keep their private hours very much under wraps, for obvious reasons. They don't take their leisure or recreation on their own patch, not if they're sensible. Mike Fletcher is sensible. Not many people know the off-duty man. But I do and McKaskill knows I do.'

'So what'll you do?'

'I don't know. It depends on what McKaskill's accumulated on me over the years. On how much of it I can weather. And I have to allow for my physical fear of the man. He's hurt people before. Dreadfully.'

A terrible thought occurred to Dermot.

'He could probably ruin you any time he felt like it,' he said.

Martin swallowed some more of his drink.

FOURTEEN

From the little room at the top of the old brewery Steve McMillan could see the street where he lived. The house itself was too far away to be distinct, but he could guess at the spot. He imagined his mother sitting there with her hands wrapped round a tea mug, waiting. He thought about her for a while and tried not to cry.

When the sadness ebbed, he took stock of his surroundings. The room wasn't much, but it was dry and warm, with a big silver-painted radiator against one wall. There was a kitchen table, a chair and a filing cabinet with no drawers. It was as much of a home as he was going to know until things changed. He didn't want to think of that time, the where or when.

He picked up a folded newspaper from the floor. It was a *Mirror*, four years old. He turned to the back automatically. The racing page put a pang across his heart. Here was an old haven, the only playground of his wits. Four meetings were tabled: Newbury, Newcastle, Market Rasen, Towcester. The going was good-to-soft at all four. He scanned the card for the North Street Handicap Chase: Vainglory, Eric the Red, Belushi, Gun Jumper, Magnifico, Falmouth Lass. He knew the form on Vainglory and Belushi: both were strong on this going, but the listed information on Gun Jumper was the best: 311-1. On the other hand it was only his second race this season and that could mean a training injury; it definitely signalled a horse with no recent battle practice. If this had been more of a specialist paper, say the *Sporting Life*, he'd have been able to dig into the nags' full form and come up with a forecast based on what he read plus what he knew, which was a lot . . .

He dropped the paper and went back to the window, reminding

himself that those days, like all the other things lopped off by his one mad act, were beyond his reach. They were gone.

He looked out across the city, feeling the old wood of the casement creak under his elbows. The sky was clouding over. There would be more rain soon. He felt a spark of gratitude for being out of the cold. And he supposed he liked the size of the room, its snugness. He felt protected. Years ago he had dreamt up a perfect room: it would be no bigger than a cupboard, lined with carpet on floor and walls, with a spotlight set in the ceiling. He could sit in there with the door locked, able to touch all four walls, and he could study form or just do nothing, all day long, without having to share his space. Daydreaming about it made him feel safe.

This room though, he began to think, could turn out to be nearly as good. If he had enough to eat and drink, a decent sleeping bag and a daily racing paper he could survive easily. He didn't need much to get by on and he never got bored. That was a bonus, he had known it since he was a boy. He could sit and let time pass without feeling he had to do anything with it.

Spots of rain tapped the window. He looked over the rooftops to where his mum would be. She was the only human being he really cared about. Terry mattered, too, but he didn't provoke caring. Mum was the source of the only kind of love Steve wanted; she was the solitary focus of his concern. Right now he wanted to know how she was. He hoped when Terry came he would tell him she was fine and not worrying too much. When Steve knew she was OK, he wouldn't have to think about her again for a while.

A fragile peace edged into his mood. Perched here above the city he felt sealed-off. He had never wanted more than this. If it wasn't for the trouble, the disaster, this would be nearly perfect.

But maybe things would work out for him the way Terry had said — if he stayed here long enough, they might stop looking for him. The world of people would leave him alone. The thought became part of the small peace. He stared out at the rain, letting time slide over him.

FIFTEEN

Percy Cullen disliked unplanned encounters, but occasionally they paid dividends. This afternoon he felt purposeful and driven by urgency, the sense of it growing as his plan hardened. It was a nuisance to be hailed in the Talisman Bar by another detective sergeant, Brian Sillitoe from North Division. On the other hand, this turned out to be an opportunity for Cullen to score points and show off his knowledge to the plebs around the bar. That was always satisfying.

Sillitoe was in the district for a court appearance. He gave his evidence early and had been in the Talisman for an hour when Cullen showed up looking for Terry McMillan, or at least a clue to his whereabouts. He drew a blank and in the process he was spotted by the lightly oiled Sillitoe, who insisted on buying him a drink.

'I was remarking to our friend here,' Sillitoe said, lolling against the bar, 'that TV programme about Jack the Ripper last night — it was a load of crap.'

'I didn't see it,' Cullen said, observing that the friend Sillitoe referred to was a mild-looking, shabby little man who had probably come in for a pint and ten minutes' peace. 'I never like to watch anything about crime or the police on the box. They always get it wrong. It annoys me.'

'This was a drama,' Sillitoe explained. 'I know they're entitled to a bit of licence when they make a play out of a case, I accept that. But this one had so many holes in it, so much pure bunkum, it was just misleading. It had nothing to do with the real Ripper case.' He ran his fingertips across his head, monitoring his crew cut. 'For a start, they made out there were seven victims.'

'Rubbish,' Cullen said to his glass.

'Right. There were six and six only.'

'Five.' Cullen looked at Sillitoe. 'Only five.'

'I think you're wrong there, Percy.'

'I'm not wrong. The only reliable source of information on the matter is the Macnaghten Papers —'

'Which aren't available yet for public perusal,' Sillitoe put in, noticing they were raising a bit of interest among the punters. 'They're locked away in the Public Record Office.'

'But some of us know what's in them,' Cullen said. 'I can tell you this without a shadow of doubt — Sir Melville Macnaghten said there were only five murders that could be put down to the Ripper.'

'That's not what I heard.'

Sillitoe looked at the half dozen men on either side. They seemed to be watching Cullen. As usual, his dogmatic tone passed for authority with people who weren't equipped to make the distinction.

'What you heard, Brian, was the same old claptrap picked up from newspaper stories at the time of the killings.' Cullen sniffed. 'It's dangerous to have opinions before you have the facts.'

'Say what you like.' Sillitoe looked huffy now. 'I know what I know.'

'False knowledge is no knowledge at all.' Cullen said it loud and clear. There was a chance here to pursue Sillitoe into a corner. 'Tell me straight, have you ever seen a transcript of the Macnaghten Papers?'

'No. I never said I had.'

'Well, I've seen them, the genuine handwritten documents, and I've read them. It's horse's-mouth stuff, Brian. The real lowdown from an Assistant Chief Constable who was there when it all happened. *Five* victims, he said. All killed out in the open except for the fifth and final one, who was croaked inside a house.' Cullen had the audience in his grip now. He swallowed some beer and put down the glass slowly. 'You being an authority, I suppose you know the names of the victims, nature of wounding, dates of crimes, all that?'

Sillitoe glared.

'I don't claim to be an expert.'

'You claimed to know better than the television people. So far, you're as wide of the mark as they were.'

'And you know all that stuff, do you — names, dates and such?'

It was a chance-everything challenge and Sillitoe realised he shouldn't have tried it. Cullen was nodding confidently a second before the gauntlet landed.

'Let me see, now,' he said, frowning hammily to call up the facts. 'As I recall, the murders were all committed between August and November, 1888.'

He looked around him with his one-sided smile.

'Is that it? Chapter and verse? Big deal,' Sillitoe said, stepping into another cowpat.

'Now, as for the victims themselves,' Cullen went on, 'let me think . . .' He closed his eyes, frowned, opened them again. 'In order of killing they were, first, Mary Ann Nichols, on August the thirty-first at Buck's Row. Then there was Annie Chapman at Hanbury Street. That was September the eighth. The third and fourth victims were killed on the same night, the thirtieth of September — Elizabeth Stride in Berner Street and Catherine Eddowes at Mitre Square. On the ninth of November Mary Jane Kelly was slaughtered in her room in Miller's Court.'

Cullen paused for a sip of beer and more dramatic effect.

'The five women,' he continued, 'all of them prostitutes, as I'm sure you know, Brian, had their throats cut. Nichols had one or two injuries to the stomach, Chapman's stomach and private parts were hacked up and long chunks of her insides were wrapped round her neck. Stride had no injuries beyond the cut throat, but Eddowes' face and belly were badly sliced up. Kelly was practically chopped to bits — there were chunks of her all over the room.'

Cullen soaked up the mutters of approbation and enjoyed Sillitoe's chapfallen look. His own expression changed as somebody spoke behind him.

'Is there any room in your head for nice things, Percy?'

He turned and saw Mike Fletcher.

'Inspector.' He delivered the rank like a blunt weapon. 'I didn't hear you creeping in.'

'I walked in,' Mike said. 'I used the sound of tumbling garbage for cover.'

Sillitoe sized up the antagonism and found its character surprising. It was easy to be anti-Cullen, but it wasn't Fletcher's style to go on the attack so brazenly. He was a classic slow burner. Or he had been. People said there were changes in him since his little girl died.

'What do you do for an encore?' Mike said, moving between the two sergeants, nodding to Sillitoe. 'The evidence from the Moors Murders trial they couldn't print? Snippets from Dennis Nilsen's diary?'

Relishing this, Sillitoe watched Cullen smother a succession of impulses. When it came to violent urges his face was a large-print book.

'I was settling an argument,' he said. 'I don't like hearing bullshit passed off as information.'

'I wasn't trying to inform anybody,' Sillitoe said. 'I was just spilling out my ignorance.'

'Weren't you just,' Cullen grunted.

Sillitoe finished his drink and stepped away from the bar.

'Got to go,' he said. 'Nice to see you, Inspector.'

'See you again,' Mike said.

Sillitoe left. Mike ordered a Grouse and took it to a table in the corner. Cullen followed him and sat down opposite.

'That was out of order,' he said.

'You were out of order when I got here. There's bound to be a regulation forbidding coppers to spout pornography at the defenceless public.'

'I was clearing up a point.'

'You were doling out a nasty, lopsided account of sadistic murder. To paint a half-way balanced picture of the Ripper case, you have to mention the grinding misery of the victims' circumstances, the unthinkable agony they went through before they died, things like that.' Mike swallowed his whisky and stared at Cullen. 'But then, dirty stories are always better if you leave out the human content, right? You don't want compassion getting in the way of titillation.'

'You're over-reacting.' Cullen said.

'Like hell I am. Listen, when I walked in here a couple of minutes ago I'd already had a bellyful of other people's sadism. The topic of your doting monologue put the tin hat on it.' Mike drummed his fingers on the table. 'How well did you know Sergeant Lowther?'

'I hardly knew him at all.'

'Well, I happen to know *he* was getting his kicks from hurting people. I've just been to the station for a chat with one or two older hands who worked with him. They didn't need any encouragement to talk. It seems Lowther was a great one for threatening villains with disaster. The special twist was, he liked prolonging the threats and adding frills until people were shitting themselves.'

'So what?' Cullen demanded. 'Villains are villains.'

'Sorry, I forgot. Rule One, suspects are fair game for twisted scuffers like Lowther any time they need a target for their perversion.'

'Jesus . . .' Cullen looked about him disgustedly. 'You're making a lot out of very little, if you'll pardon me saying.'

'The fewer a man's principles,' Mike said, 'the feebler his perception of outrage.'

'Who's that?' Cullen sneered. 'Shakespeare?'

'No. It's Mike Fletcher. Just one of the little aphorisms I concoct now and then as an alternative to despair. But I'm digressing.' Mike put his hands on the table and lowered his head an inch. 'I just learned, among other things, that Sergeant Lowther hounded a girl for two months until she turned herself in on a till-thieving rap.'

'So? Plodding police work isn't a sin, is it?'

'No. But torture is. By the time she showed up at the station her life had been made intolerable. Anxiety and pure fear had turned her into a wreck. And guess what? She was innocent. The manageress at the shop where she worked admitted the whole thing, as soon as she heard about the confession. She'd been at it for months and she could prove she had. Lowther had been getting his jollies victimising the girl — the question of guilt didn't come into it.'

'Is there any point to all this, Inspector? I've things to do.'

'Bear with me, Percy. I made my enquiries about Lowther on the basis of evidence that he was playing a very ugly nerve game with Steve McMillan.'

'What evidence?'

'Something I picked up, the source isn't important.'

Cullen made a visible mental note.

'I believe now that it's true,' Mike went on. 'Lowther was torturing McMillan. But this case was different. Lowther knew his days as a copper, and probably as a human being, were numbered.'

'Something else you picked up?'

'That's right. What do you reckon to the theory of him playing his game to the absolute limit, going all the way, knowing there was nothing at all to lose? What about him deliberately driving the kid to attack him, maybe even kill him?'

'I'd say a theory like that would throw doubt on the sanity of the person who came up with it.'

'Keep your words sweet, Percy. You never know when you'll have to eat them.'

Cullen stood up and pushed back the chair.

'There's one more thing,' Mike said. 'A memo for you. Lay off Mrs McMillan.'

'What does that mean?'

'You know what it means. No more threats. Just leave her alone, she can't help us find Steve. Or Terry.'

Cullen gripped the back of the chair and leaned forward.

'If anybody was to ask me right now, Inspector, I'd say you were going all out to protect that bunch.'

'No,' Mike said, 'it isn't like that at all. I'm not shielding the McMillans. I'm impeding you.'

'Are you saying I've behaved improperly?'

'That's what I'm saying. In my view you're a walking impropriety.'

'You'll hear more about this.' Cullen straightened his rugger-club tie. 'Wait and see.'

'I'll wait, Percy,' Mike said, watching him go.

SIXTEEN

The woman came from the desk-sergeant's office carrying a half-full polythene sack. She looked around uncertainly, then headed along the corridor, reading doorplates as she went. Mike saw her as he came away from the coffee dispenser. He guessed she was in her early forties, wearing tinted, big-frame glasses to camouflage her eye-lines. Her coat was beige wool with a broad yellow scarf wound under the collar. As she came nearer, Mike caught her perfume.

'Can I help at all?'

She stopped and looked at him. Mike gave her a tight-lipped smile. The coffee cup was scalding his fingers.

'You're Mr Fletcher.'

'That's right.'

'You won't remember me. I'm Diane Lowther.'

Click. He had met her at a Christmas social, two or three years before.

'Of course,' he said, nodding. 'It would be daft to ask how you are . . .'

'Ah, well . . .' She made a little mouth and held up the bag. 'Some belongings they asked me to collect,' she said. 'Bits and pieces out of his locker.'

'I'm sure that could have waited.'

'I don't mind. It's something to do.'

Mike pointed at the big dented dispenser.

'Let me get you a coffee or something.'

She hesitated, then said she would like that. Mike led her to the machine, put down his own cup and filled a fresh one.

'I've never been here before,' she said, looking around.

'Grubby.' Mike handed her the coffee. 'But it's home. Let's sit in here for a minute. You look tired.'

They went into an empty interview room and sat at opposite sides of the table, leaving the door open. Mike offered her a cigarette. She took it with unsteady fingers. They lit up and sat back, looking at each other. Mike asked if the press had been giving her a hard time.

'No, oddly enough. They got hold of my husband's address from somewhere, but nobody's given them mine. So far.'

'They'll find you,' Mike sighed. 'They're everywhere. There's even a handful camped out in reception.'

'I saw them. They didn't catch on to who I am.' Mrs Lowther looked at the plastic bag. 'I've to see the superintendent next. I suppose he wants to offer his personal condolences.'

'I'll show you his office in a minute.'

Mrs Lowther put an elbow on the table and tilted her head at Mike.

'My husband didn't like you. Did you know that?'

'I'd no idea he took any notice of me.'

'Oh, he did. That's why I'd no trouble recognising you. You were prominent on George's list of soft-centred men. The list got longer every week.' Mrs Lowther smiled. 'Don't be embarrassed by me. I'm very direct about things. I teach thirteen-to-fifteen-year-olds, which makes a person good at externalising everything. I'm also full of Valium, which tends to induce candour.'

She shifted in her chair, recrossed her legs, drew deeply on her cigarette.

'I remember the dance when we were introduced. George slotted everybody into a category for me that night — they were Sound, Unsound, Hard, Soft and so on. His classifications of other policemen tightened in the last year we were together.'

'How long were you separated?'

'Ten months. I ended up on the list too, you see. Soft. I reasoned with savages when I should have been instilling a healthy fear of authority.' She paused. 'George despised me.'

Mike looked down at his cup.

'I'm shocking you, am I?'

'No. I'm just . . . surprised.'

'Maybe relief's making me talk this way. Or the vengeful impulse. After the first jolt, when they told me he was dead, I couldn't resist thinking — he won't be round to take it out on me ever again. Lately, he enjoyed hurting me.'

'He was ill.'

'I know. For a while I told myself that excused it. But he didn't leave any chinks for my sympathy.' Mrs Lowther shook herself and sat up in the chair. 'I'm rambling. It *is* the Valium.'

'I wonder . . .' Mike cleared his throat, started again. 'If this is impertinent, forgive me, but I'd like to know — did your husband's illness exclude hope? I mean he lived for the job, so had he made plans for when he would have to retire? Or was he shutting the notion out?'

Mrs Lowther considered the question.

'George had decided he was dying,' she said. 'That was all. And two weeks ago, the last time I saw him, he told me his death would be the ruin of more than just him. I thought he was turning insane. I'm afraid I still think that. He was going mad on a mediaeval scale.'

Mike tented his hands. Mrs Lowther drank some coffee.

'Maybe I should go and see the superintendent now,' she said, putting down the cup.

'I'll show you where to find him.'

Outside Foster's office Mrs Lowther thanked Mike for the coffee.

'There's one thing more I'd like to tell you,' she said. 'I suppose I've been aware of it since I woke up this morning.'

'What?'

'Well, whoever it was that killed George . . . I admit I don't know many of the details, but even so, I think I'm a bit sorry for that man.'

A thick smell of decay wafted off hillocks of fly-tipped garbage on the spare ground behind the McMillans' house. It made Percy Cullen's stomach lurch, but he was obliged to stand downwind because the only cover was this corrugated-iron lean-to against the back of the house. He breathed carefully, grateful it wasn't summer. His feet felt dead with the cold and there was a pain in his back from standing hunched too long in the shadows.

He had been there for more than an hour. There was no alternative, this was his final option. Elsewhere there was no trace of Terry McMillan. When hunting failed to get a result you tried waiting instead, and if you picked your spot cunningly enough your quarry would come straight to you. Sometimes.

It was after four and getting dark. Time was short. Cullen had to bite down on his impatience. He wanted victory on this one, a flash of glory, and not only for the satisfaction of shitting all over Mike Fletcher. This case was different, like the superintendent said. It had to be brought to conclusion by a high-profile cop with a ballsy style and the stamp of the avenger on him. The Steve McMillan arrest had to be Cullen's. For sure.

'Come on, you little bastard,' he hissed, watching the tendrils of his breath steam away on darkening air.

The urgency he felt earlier had transmuted to clamp-jawed determination. It had a lot to do with the superintendent's faith in him. And with Fletcher lecturing him in the pub, putting him down like that. He really thought he was something, that Fletcher. The thought of him put a gripe in Cullen's gut.

There was an unbidden segment of memory. He saw Barbara Fletcher, luminously naked in the dark, goading him beyond natural limits with her atavism, her spread legs, her frantic fingers. *All of it, Percy, give me all of it!*'

If only the adventure had ended there, on a high note, with Cullen as exultant cuckolder, a DS banging a DI's estranged wife. But Fletcher had had his last word as usual, his sneering deflation. *She's done the rounds since she was kicked out, Percy. But you've never been fussy about who you mix yours with, have you?* Triumph in the head had turned to ashes in Cullen's mouth. Victory died aborning. Again.

But that was all set to change. Cullen had the superintendent on his team. Between them they could cut the feet from Fletcher.

'Come *on* . . .'

Terry still hadn't been home to see his mother. She was frantic and Terry would know she was. He wouldn't be able to stay away.

With a visible police presence in the street the only way he could hope to get in was from the back. So where was he?

The thought occurred that he might have done a runner. Cullen kicked the notion aside. It was no use dwelling on barriers. Believing that Terry was still in the district provided the only realistic hope of finding Steve McMillan soon.

Minutes passed. It got colder and the smell off the rubbish seemed to get worse. Cullen wasn't curious enough to try fathoming that, he just wished it wasn't so. He began to think about Mrs McMillan again. Maybe she knew more than she was saying. He doubted it, but he could go up there again, lean on her harder . . .

There was a sound. Cullen crouched. It could have been a dog, he thought, or a scavenging cat. Another couple of soft rustles, then a figure appeared. He was crouched, too, taking a serpentine route through the trash. Cullen peered and confirmed. It was *him*. Terry McMillan. The ferret on a homing run.

Cullen edged out, away from the lean-to, bending lower and spreading his arms. When Terry was two yards away he swung like a crab and gripped the boy's shoulder.

'Terence. Welcome home.'

Terry spun away. He wriggled, kicked. Cullen hit him twice on the ear with the flat of his hand, wrenched him round and backhanded him on the mouth. Terry gulped and sagged to his knees. Cullen put a hand on each shoulder, holding Terry in position. He aimed with the pointed toe of his shoe and kicked forward sharply. The shoe hit Terry's groin with a sound like a hammer thudding on a pillow. The boy grunted and heaved ominously. Cullen stepped back to let him vomit. Terry retched three times and disgorged all the food he had eaten that day. He reeled back from the puddle between his knees and tried to stand. Cullen took him by the hair. He drove three sharp punches into his belly and waited for Terry to stop moaning.

'You can go when I know where your brother is.'

Terry wiped his swelling lips with his sleeve.

'I don't know where he went,' he panted, trembling with nausea and pain.

'Try again.'

'Honest.'

'You'll tell me,' Cullen promised. 'If I've to kick your balls off you'll tell me.'

Terry took several deep breaths. His whole body shuddered.

'How can I tell you where he is when I don't know?'

'Right,' Cullen snapped. 'If that's the way you want it.'

He went behind Terry, hoisted him by the armpits and dragged him to the nearest pile of garbage. He thrust the boy forward and pushed his face deep into the mush, pinning him with his foot. He grasped Terry's arm and twisted it behind his back, forcing the elbow out and up toward the shoulder. Terry roared against the filth clogging his mouth. Cullen kept up the pressure, levering the arm higher until he felt the shoulder give way. He stepped back. Terry's head jerked up, gulping air, every laboured breath a moan. One-handed, like a puppet with a string gone, he pushed himself to his knees. Cullen stepped close.

'What do you have to say now?'

Terry tried to speak.

'I'm waiting, son. But I can't wait long. This is urgent.' He prodded the ruined shoulder, making Terry whimper. 'Tell me.'

'Brewery,' Terry gasped.

'Eh?'

'Machin's . . . Steve's there.'

'Whereabouts?'

'The top. A little room.'

'He's on his own?'

Terry nodded weakly.

'You know what'll happen if you're lying to me?'

'He's there, honest he is.'

'Fine. Well done.'

'Don't hurt him,' Terry moaned. 'He won't . . .' He stopped, coughed. 'He won't give you any trouble. Just don't hit him or anything . . .'

Cullen stepped back, brushing his hands together.

'I told you you'd tell me where he is, didn't I? You could have made it a lot easier for yourself. You tough guys are all the same —

everything's got to be the hard way.' He put his face close to Terry's. 'Do I have to warn you to say nothing about this meeting of ours?'

'No.'

'Not ever? To anybody? Do I need to tell you what the *real* hard way could be like?'

'No,' Terry panted.

'There's a good little chap.'

Cullen moved away, picking his way carefully through the rubbish. Swaying, Terry watched him.

'Don't hurt Steve. Please . . .'

SEVENTEEN

Kate Barbour switched on the light above the bed. Mike blinked at her from the pillow. He reached out to touch the burnish of sweat on her shoulder.

'Now I understand why you knocked off early,' she said. 'That was definitely an emergency.'

'You know me and my glands. All swash and buckle.'

Kate ruffled his hair. She liked these aftermaths, the nerveless, calm passages when she could watch him smoke, listen to his breathing, touch him. If there was regret, it was that the intense closeness they reached in the dark was gone. Nothing else was like that. For Kate, certainly, nothing ever had been. Yet they did no unusual things in bed. They felt no need for erotic specialities; the simplest contacts and movements delighted them. Kate had wondered at that, remembering elaborate sexual experiences with earlier lovers, occasions that had never generated the kind of raptures she knew when she made love with Mike Fletcher. She had stopped wondering about it one night when Mike said he and she were a physical and emotional match. It was weak aetiology — but this was life, not psychiatry, so she needed no better explanation.

'Why *did* you get here so early?' she said, watching him rest the ashtray on his chest and light up a Rothmans. 'You haven't pulled in Steve McMillan yet. I thought that meant working late.'

'It should, I suppose. But we don't have much of a chance at night. Wherever his hideout is, it's a good one. Either he'll have to come out before we catch him, or somebody will have to tell us where he is.' Under the rumpled duvet he reached for Kate's thigh and squeezed it gently. 'So I thought, why waste my time on the cold streets? I might as well be having a bit of therapy with my friendly shrink.'

'Do you feel better?'

'Nearly cured.'

Kate looked thoughtful for a minute.

'I think I'll have a brandy,' she said. 'Fancy one?'

'I'd love one.'

Mike watched her climb out of bed, dainty in her nakedness as she got the bottle and two glasses from a chest of drawers by the window. They only ever drank brandy in the bedroom, and only after they made love.

'A large one, to put back your strength.'

She handed him the drink and scrambled back into bed with her own. They clinked glasses and sipped.

'I haven't asked you lately,' Kate said, 'how have you been sleeping?'

'About the same, I suppose. I still get the dooms if I don't drop off straight away.'

She had told him he should talk about it more, but it depressed him to do that. So he said. But Kate knew he could handle depression and any other nerve-brain dysfunction. What he couldn't hack was the encroachment of pain on his spirit. In that territory he was seriously wounded. Even attempts at healing made him suffer. He resisted every effort to make him talk out his grief, he refused to air it and start the process of mending. Which didn't mean, Kate believed, that she or anybody else should stop trying.

'Moira's been dead for just over a year,' she ventured. 'If everything was going the way it should, you'd be able to think about her without feeling so bad.'

'I'll be all right,' he said, firmly enough to block her inroad. 'Things will fall into place. Time'll see to it — I need more time than most people, that's all.'

Kate wanted to argue. She swallowed some brandy instead. Whatever he said about letting matters be, she knew the wound was festering. Time, unabetted, would make it worse. The grief of losing Moira had struck him when he was already suffering — Barbara had finally gone, taking with her all their savings and leaving Mike with an ulcerous gap where his trust had nestled. His daughter, a beguiling Pre-Raphaelite fifteen-year-old, had been his treasure, his consolation for the wasted years with his wife. Losing Moira to septicaemia, from a simple scratch at that, had devastated him. Now, under his various surfaces, the pain burned on. At times Kate couldn't help interfering, but most of the time she knew she had to wait until Mike admitted he needed help.

'I've news,' he said. 'I know what gave Steve McMillan the drive to go for Lowther the way he did.'

'What?'

'His fear.'

'What was he afraid of?'

'The unknown. The pit of blackest, nameless possibilities.'

Kate looked blank.

'Lowther was terrorising him,' Mike said.

'How?'

'With dire threats, ominous promises. He was keeping the kid off balance and driving him to the edge. Our dead sergeant was another sociopath. Probably suicidal with it. There's room for arguing that he was trying to drive Steve to attack him.'

'Fear would do it,' Kate said slowly. 'Extreme fear. There's a lot been written about it, mostly in midbrain studies carried out here and in America.'

'Midbrain?'

'The primitive part of the brain. The *reptilian* component. It doesn't get involved in reasoning, it simply reacts to basic stimuli like hunger and danger. It's essentially self-preserving.'

'Sounds highly sci-fi.'

'Pure sci,' Kate said, 'no fi. Usually the midbrain's inert, but there's evidence that in some people the snake element goes active when the other parts of the brain, the reasoning parts, come under too much pressure. They can get overloaded by fright, or terror more likely, especially if they haven't been too stable or well-developed to begin with.'

'And then the reptilian part takes over?'

'Right. And it's purely reactive. It perceives the problem then takes direct measures, no matter how extreme, to cancel it.'

'The way a rattlesnake does.'

Kate nodded.

'It's reckoned that a lot of really outstanding heroes were under exclusive influence of the midbrain when they did the crazy mad brave things that got them their medals. They did what they did because they were frightened in the absolute extreme.'

'What happened to Steve had to be extreme,' Mike said. 'I've talked to people who knew Lowther's style. Fear was his weapon of choice. One copper told me he'd chase a mouse into a corner and play scary tactics with it for minutes before he'd kill it. I've spoken to his widow, too. The consensus seems to be that under the helmet with the nice shiny badge, Lowther was a psychotic dinosaur.'

'Could you prove that?'

'In mitigation?' Mike nodded slowly. 'I think so.'

'But it was still murder, wasn't it?'

'I think manslaughter would stand a chance as a plea, even though the victim was a copper. And the evidence of an articulate psychiatrist would help to soften a jury's options.'

Kate shifted closer, let her hand rest on his stomach.

'I'm glad you said that. I was having bad feelings about Steve.'

Mike looked at her.

'What kind of bad feelings?'

'The inadequate kind. Borderline guilt. The kind I get when cases go from bad to worse, in spite of my expert intervention.'

'That's what you reckon, is it? You're inadequate?' Mike squeezed her thigh again. 'At the risk of making you go all pink, I've got to say you've a reputation for being a hotshot.'

Kate set her shoulders against the headboard.

'It's the shortcomings of psychiatry itself that bother me,' she said. 'See, I don't trust basic procedures, even. Take the psychiatric interview . . .'

'You're going to talk shop,' Mike said. 'But go ahead. What's the psychiatric interview?'

'The first meeting with a patient. The idea is to establish a good doctor-patient relationship. At the same time we try to get enough information to lay down a diagnosis and sketch a course of treatment.'

'You don't go along with that?' Mike said over the rim of his glass.

'In principle I do. But the interview can bring out the worst in a shrink. The tendency is to analyse *everything* and run it through the professional checklist — what the patient says, how he says it, his pattern of eye-movement, how his body behaves while he's talking. Normal values go out the window.'

'To clarify,' Mike said.

'OK. An example.' Kate smoothed the duvet. 'During a seminar I was at last year, I talked to a consultant at one of the coffee breaks. We chatted about this and that and eventually we got around to cases. I gave him an outline of a certain man's interview behaviour. I described his repetitive speech pattern, his hesitant delivery and the agitated body language he used while he was talking to me. I detailed everything and asked him what he thought. He listened, mulled it over, then told me the man probably had a chronic affective disorder.'

'What's that?'

'A disturbance of affect is when anxiety or depression or even elation inflates itself into a disorder. Do you follow me?'

'I think so,' Mike said.

'OK. So I asked the consultant if he thought his own moods were in whack. He gave me a funny look and said yes, of course they were, he'd be no good at his job if they weren't. So then I confessed I'd just described his behaviour the very first time I met him.'

'Nice one.'

'He went apeshit. He accused me of unprofessional jokery, said my flippancy was unbecoming in a professional, all the defensive stuff. When he settled down I told him I was making a point — psychiatrists tend to find disturbances in areas where none exist. They get into the habit of mistaking idiosyncrasy for disorder.'

'Is there a remedy?'

'Sure. Less of the analysis and a lot more straightforward human judgement. It's easy to say, not so easy to do when you're conditioned the way we are.'

'What's all this to do with you feeling you've let Steve McMillan down?'

'Nothing,' Kate said. 'Anybody can see what's wrong with Steve. Even a psychiatrist.'

'So?'

'I was giving you an example of a fundamental procedure which I happen to think is dodgy. What bothers me *most* about the job, though, is the quality of treatment. Half the time it's unsound, or feeble, or counterproductive. Steve was sent to me by the court because he showed signs of a chronic mood disorder that left him open to criminal influences. So what could I do?'

'You're asking me?'

'I'm asking myself. He didn't respond well to talking, in fact it was a struggle to get anything out of him. I mean a *struggle*. So after a while I considered electroplexy.'

'Which is?'

'The shock box. It used to be called ECT — electro-convulsive therapy, except nowadays there's no convulsion. The patient's given a muscle relaxant, then he gets a split-second burst of electricity across his brain. It's a treatment that can have highly successful effects.'

'Did you use it on Steve?'

'No. I don't often use it at all.'

'Why not?'

'Because the technique's been around in one form or another since the eighteenth century and we still don't know why it works.' Kate flapped her hand on the duvet. 'It's like bloody witchcraft. In Steve's case I was worried it might affect him badly — there are features of his personality that raised the possibility of an adverse reaction.'

Mike took a slow sip of brandy, nodding.

'So I thought about drugs,' Kate said. 'But not for long. With somebody like him, drugs can produce a replica of the undead.' She sighed. 'In the end I decided to keep on chatting to him, session after session, which was like talking to a potato. The whole up and down of it is, I didn't do a thing for Steve.'

'But you tried.'

'From what you tell me, the man he killed had a thousand times more effect on his personality than I ever did. Yet I'm supposed to be an expert . . .'

'You don't use fear, Kate. You don't threaten and scare. That kind of stuff gets results without any training.'

Kate sank down on the pillow.

'It was a dumb thing for me to say. File it under Blurred Reasoning, and in brackets put, Result of Anxiety Concerning Professional Shortcomings.'

'Consider it done.'

Mike placed his glass on the cabinet by the bed. He took Kate's drink and put it beside his own. Rolling on his side to face her, he put one arm round her waist and gently stroked her back.

'Hold on to this thought,' he said. 'In court, you can do Steve a power of good.'

'Mm.' Kate nuzzled his shoulder. 'Nice thought.'

They kissed. Her hand glided round his hip and down into his groin. She pulled back and stared at him, eyes theatrically wide.

'That brandy's better than I thought,' she said.

'It's not the brandy.'

He kissed her throat. She moved down, accepting the gentle insistence of his weight.

'What is it, then?'

'All this psychiatric talk. Freud reckoned most psychological conflicts are grounded in sex, didn't he? So, by extension, discussing psychiatry can be the same as talking about sex.'

'Yes. If you want to reason along such twisted lines.'

'Oh, I do.'

His hand shaped itself to her buttock.

'I love it when you talk dirty,' he said.

EIGHTEEN

The dramatic possibilities of night-time were not lost on Percy Cullen. Dawn raids could be sensational, too, but with them it was the element of surprise that gave him a charge, seeing the fuddled, startled, *caught* look on the villains' faces. Night swoops were more than that, they were special. Percy couldn't analyse it, he never tried to analyse anything. He simply knew it made him feel like he was in a movie or something. There was an element of the heroic in nabbing somebody at dead of night.

Standing on the second landing from the top of the brewery stairs, he got another of his memory flashes. A house, three in the morning, himself and two DCs, come to grab a pusher shacked up with his teenage girlfriend. They had burst into the bedroom, Cullen hitting the light switch. The pair were in bed, coming awake, bleary, grunting. She was a cracker, raven-haired, naked under the covers with one breast exposed. Cullen hauled the man out of bed and told the other two to take him to the kitchen and hold him. When they went out it took him a second, no longer, to grab the bedclothes off the fear-stiffened girl and have a look. He could still see her; firm tits, wide smooth hips, athletic thighs with a compelling black tuft at the junction. She was very, very scared. Cullen grabbed her by the backs of her knees, drew her across the mattress and spread her. 'Looking for dope, love,' he said, loud enough for the others to hear, and slid a finger into her vagina, warning her with his eyes. She felt slick. They had been doing it. The hairy bastard in the kitchen had been up her. If things had been different, if the other two had been outside the house waiting, Percy would have cuffed the man, put him in the kitchen and gone back to the girl. He'd have shoved *his* cock up there, right to the hilt — her word against his, no sweat. But at least he copped a feel, whipped out his dick and made her touch it, then it was, 'Come on, love, wrap the quilt round your shoulders, into the kitchen with you . . .'

Now he peered up the brewery stairs, locating the door in the gloom. A big moment, this. He was on the brink of pulling off a high-profile job, the collar that would put his picture in the papers and fanfare his promotion. And he was on his own. The slimy punk behind that door up there was all his. The tingly feeling came. He began to climb again, on his toes.

At the door he checked the luminous face of his watch. Two-twenty. An unguarded time, even for the fugitive, the frantic. Percy curled his fingers round the doorknob, squeezed and turned it a fraction, paused, turned another fraction, paused, another fraction. It clicked softly. He pushed the door open an inch, put his ear to the gap. There was steady breathing in the dark. He reached for his torch, got his thumb on the button. The breathing stopped. He heard rustling movement.

'Who's there?' a young voice said, tremulous. 'Terry? Is that you?'

Cullen threw open the door and stamped into the room. He flicked on the torch and saw Steve straight away, curled in the corner with an anorak over him.

'No, it's not Terry.' Cullen felt on the wall beside him and found the light switch. 'Not your fairy godmother, either.' The bare bulb came on, making Steve wrinkle his eyes. 'On your feet, fuckface.'

Steve slid upright, his back pressed to the corner. His face was sick-pale, wrecked-looking. There were greenish patches under his eyes.

'So you're the one.' Cullen took two steps towards Steve and stopped, eyes narrowed. 'You're the big bad killer. I can't say I'm impressed, Steve. You look like shit.'

Steve swallowed dryly.

'Are you going to put up a fight, tough guy? Going to have a go at putting the boot in?'

Cullen was tingling top to bottom. The fear he saw, the cowering near-terror, made it stronger. His balls felt tight.

97

Steve dropped the anorak he had been clutching. He bent to retrieve it.

'Uh, oh, trying it on, eh?'

Cullen stepped forward and smacked Steve on the side of the head. Steve let go the anorak and stiffened against the wall. Cullen punched him in the stomach. Steve gasped and doubled over.

'Trying to resist arrest — that's serious, Tiger. I'm entitled to stop you doing that.'

'I'm not —'

Cullen took a handful of Steve's hair and threw him against the opposite wall. His face hit the side of the window frame. Cullen was hopping from foot to foot, boosted. Steve had his back to him, clutching his injured face, whimpering.

'You're scum, McMillan. Filth.'

Steve groaned as a punch landed over his kidney. The other fist slammed the back of his head, banged his face on the frame again. He turned, blood welling from his nose. His eyes were deranged, terrified beyond sanity. He came at Cullen, arms outstretched.

'That's right, that's right . . .'

Cullen drew back his right fist and shot it forward. The impact with Steve's chin jolted along his arm. Steve fell back on the low window ledge. Cullen panted, crouched. He was burning now, ablaze, a vengeful engine. None of this was planned, but it wasn't to be resisted.

'Attack *me*, would you? Do I look like your size of target, you crummy fucker?'

Teeth set, eyes as wild as his victim's, Cullen closed in. He punched Steve's bulk across the width of the ledge, catching him on the chest, the shoulder, the neck.

'Pig bastard shit!'

Cullen wound up for another volley. Steve tried to scramble back. He was bleeding, whimpering, out of himself again in the terrible world of danger and pain. His back was against the window. He put his hands up over his face as Cullen's flying fists landed on him, banging his ribs like mallets. Behind Steve something creaked. Then it gave. He suddenly had space. He shuffled himself back, hearing glass break somewhere, and fell out into free dark space.

Cullen stared at the gap where the window had been. The whole outer frame was gone. Distantly he heard a thump. This hadn't been planned, either. He stood breathing through his mouth, panting from his exertions.

'Christ.'

He stepped back from the window, thoughts swirling. It began to dawn on him. The truth of it. The sharp, blinding fact. He had done it at last. He had avenged the ultimate crime. In full measure. He, Percy Cullen.

He gazed at the black square of night beyond the window. A minute passed, and another, soundless, then a soothing mantle of calm began to descend on him.

NINETEEN

Mike knew it was a dream, but the two-faced persuasion of sleep made him just as sure the experience was real. He was on the wonder island and Moira was with him, as she had been twice in the year before the birthday she never quite reached.

They were on the beach at El Golfo on Lanzarote, gazing out past the miraculous emerald lake to a ragged obelisk of peninsular rock being thrashed by Atlantic waves. Black sand warmed the soles of their sandalled feet. The sun was directly overhead; already it had bleached Moira's hair pale gold and darkened her skin. She looked at Mike and smiled. Language was deficient here, it couldn't express the way they felt about the place. Sensations of perfection were conveyed between them in smiles and shared gazing silences.

Developers were ruining the south and south east, but there was still an abundance of mute volcanoes, winding hill roads, unspoilt villages, olive groves, spectacular mountain caves and beaches where they walked for miles without seeing another soul.

'It's what I'd like heaven to be like,' Moira said on their first visit. 'Imagine your soul being free here for ever and ever.'

She was a romantic. Delightfully so. Standing on the spiralling road above Haria, a valley town of spotless green-and-white houses with a palm tree in every garden, she had almost cried. At Mirador del Rio, looking across a turquoise channel to the tan-and-white island of La Graciosa, she moaned at the sight, at the heart-clutching beauty.

On this warm beach, standing close to his beloved daughter, Mike was aware that early as it was, they had done a lot this dream morning. They had eaten a breakfast of fresh fruit and buttered croissants, sitting on their balcony overlooking the fishing harbour. They had cleaned the apartment then gone into the Old Town to shop for bread and meat at the *supermercado*. After a walk around the harbour, they spent half an hour watching old men gut fearful-looking fish on tables along the sea wall. Then they climbed the hill to Fred's Bar for strong coffee and the sharp repartee of the owner's sons, Jim and Peter, who entertained without patronising, a distinction noted gratefully by wise Moira.

Finally they had driven out here, to the windy warm stretches of El Golfo, to do no more than stand and stare and smile. The shimmer of the dream day was *real*, no question. As Moira turned and smiled again, Mike saw the light of sun and sea on her skin and in her amber eyes. He found it all, suddenly, too rich to contain. He sat up sharply out of his sleep, moaning.

The sensations of the dream reverberated as he climbed out of bed and got his robe from the bathroom. In Kate's tidy kitchen he put on the kettle and spooned instant coffee into a mug. It was 6.35, still dark outside and raining. Mike peered at the street lamps studding the blackness and sighed.

When the kettle boiled he poured hot water in the mug, added sugar, sat down, sipped, and wondered what category of wimp or creep he belonged to. What kind of father, subjected to the obscenity of outliving his own child, could not grieve decently, or rail against fate, or curse God, or go quietly or noisily mad? What manner of coward refused, most of the time, to face the loss square-on, and pretended, in the vividness of his dreams, that she still lived?

Barbara — brittle, fiercely pragmatic — had handled the bereavement far better. She and Moira had often quarrelled and after the break-up they didn't speak, but there was a bond nevertheless, one that hurt terribly at the breaking. Barbara spent a month swamped with grief, then began steadily to get better. There would always be a scar, but it was a spot where clean healing had taken place.

Because of flaws of character or courage, Mike had chosen to keep Moira's death from his heart, to try holding his emotions in a state that pre-dated the loss. That meant lying to himself, cutting short his awareness, concocting sentimental technicolour dreams. He could *say* Moira was dead and in all truth he knew it, but the knowledge was not allowed past certain barriers. That, he decided, was despicable.

Sitting at the kitchen table, smelling the hot coffee, he thought of those two holidays in Lanzarote. The cost of the second one had crippled his bank account, had in fact put it on crutches. But having been there he was desperate to go again, and so was Moira. They had even talked of one day having a place of their own on the island, where she could take friends and he could go alone, or with her, or with whoever he might love at some time in the future.

Oh, they had adored Lanzarote. But now he couldn't bear the thought of ever going again. The memories were too precious to supersede. One concession to the fact of Moira's death was his wish-dream that she had been consigned there; he, pathetic clown, had tried to imagine her soul roaming free and happy on the hills and shores of a distant island.

The clock on the wall buzzed its quarter-hour warning. Kate would be awake soon. He swallowed the dregs of coffee and went to the bathroom. He washed, shaved, brushed his teeth and tried to do something with his hair. In the bedroom, moving quietly, he took a fresh shirt and pants from the laundered supply he kept there and went to the sitting room to dress. When he came back, the light was on and Kate was sitting up, glue-eyed.

'Stay put,' he said. 'I'll bring you a cuppa.'

'Gawd bless you, guv.'

While Kate was in the tub he rang the station desk and asked if there were any messages. Nothing, the sergeant said, but he might be interested to know that a constable had apprehended Terry McMillan. The kid was in a bad way and they'd taken him along to the hospital. He was still there. No, nobody had questioned him yet, because he was put under sedation as soon as he arrived at the hospital.

Mike went to the bathroom and opened the door a crack. Kate whined at the draught.

'I've got to go.'

'Can't you stop and have breakfast?'

'No time. I'll borrow a brolly — the butch one, OK?'

'What's so important?'

'I don't know. That's what I'm going to find out.'

'Keep me posted if it's anything to do with Steve McMillan, will you?'

'Definitely.'

On the wet street he decided a brisk walk would be a good thing. Exercise in the drizzly cold might clear his head. If it dispersed the cobwebby traces of dreams it would be benefit enough.

The duty surgeon's office was small and tidy. On the wall was a drug manufacturer's calendar with a reproduction of Rembrandt's *The Anatomy Lesson of Dr Nicholaes Tulp*. The surgeon himself, Mr Lipman, short and skinny with red hair and lively blue eyes, looked too young to be using knives on sick people.

'The lad says he slipped on the pavement and put his shoulder out,' he told Mike.

'What do you think?'

'Somebody tortured him.'

'Torture?'

'I'm as sure as I can be,' Lipman said, 'without having been there when it happened.'

'What if somebody just twisted his arm too hard?'

'The injury would have been different.' Mr Lipman tapped his own shoulder. 'It isn't a simple dislocation. There's tearing in the ligament, which suggests a levering action, slow and deliberate. It would have to be done while the rest of the body was immobilised. The damage on the inner surface of the pectoralis major muscle . . .' he pointed into his armpit, '. . . just here, indicates powerful torsion, not a jerk or a simple twist. The coracobrachialis muscle is torn, too. That's a deep structure, it wouldn't give way from mere twisting. He was tortured, all right.'

'How is he?'

'In pain. He's sedated, but he still hurts. Apart from the job that was done on his shoulder, he's got extensive bruising on the abdomen, maybe even a bruised liver — which is why we don't want to give him any powerful painkillers just yet. His face is a bit of a mess, too.'

'Can I talk to him?'

Mr Lipman made a face.

'Five minutes,' he said.

Terry was propped up in bed with his arm strapped out to the side on an angled metal splint. There were patchy bruises on his face, and his lips were swollen and split. Mrs McMillan was sitting by the bed, gaunt and red-eyed. Mike nodded to her. She nodded back. There was nothing to say.

'I told you to be careful,' Mike said to Terry.

Terry moved his mouth to say something. He couldn't.

'Do you want to tell me who did this?'

Terry shrugged the undamaged shoulder.

'I don't need to ask. But at least tell me this much — did you tell him where Steve is?'

No response.

'Come on, Terry, you know it's important.'

Terry shut his eyes, put his head back on the pillow. Mike saw a tear slip past one eyelid. He patted the boy's hand. The cobwebs of dreams hadn't entirely gone. He felt his throat thicken, a response to youth mindlessly harmed.

'Never mind, son,' he said. 'I'll try and square things for you. For the three of you.'

TWENTY

At two minutes past one, Martin Reynolds opened his front door and admitted Guy McKaskill. They went to the sitting room, where Dermot Calder lounged on the Castrofilippo couch, one leg curled under him, the other stretched straight and elegant, the heel of his calfskin loafer submerged in the carpet pile. He stared at McKaskill with cautious disdain.

'Having a day off?' McKaskill said, addressing Martin.

'Why do you ask?'

'You're both in your casuals.'

'How observant.'

Martin and Dermot wore identical blue sea-island cotton shirts, open at the neck. Dermot had on a fawn cashmere v-neck sweater and muscle-hugging Italian jeans. A dark blue cardigan was slung over Martin's shoulders, matching his slacks and the soft indigo leather of his boots.

'I have no cases in court today,' Martin explained. 'No clients to see, either. My secretary is dealing with the office work. On days like this I like to stay home and write personal letters, or simply lounge around.'

He pointed to a chair and McKaskill sat down. His boxy charcoal suit and russet tie looked out of place. He spread his feet and fixed his eyes on Dermot.

'You a lawyer too?' he said.

Dermot shook his head and turned his face to the window.

'He's a dancer,' Martin said, pouring coffee for McKaskill.

'Ballet?'

'Theatrical,' Dermot snapped.

'Spiritually close to the mighty Astaire, I'd say.' Martin put the delicate cup and saucer on the table beside McKaskill and set milk and a sugar bowl beside them. 'But a man has to be practical, isn't that so, Dermot?' Martin crinkled his eyes at McKaskill. 'He may be an Astaire in his heart, but in performance he has to favour the broader acrobatic styles — Alvin Ailey, Wayne Sleep. It's the only way for a hoofer to make a living in show business these days.'

Martin went to his chair and sat down with measured casualness. He was nervous, working hard to keep it from showing. The civilised veneer might not hold, but the longer it did, he believed, the less distressing this encounter would be.

'Fascinating,' McKaskill said. He glared his distaste at Dermot before switching his eyes to Martin. 'Well, then. What have you got for me?'

'You mean will I tell you how and where Mike Fletcher spends time alone?'

'That's what I mean.'

'I'm not sure I really know . . .'

McKaskill had picked up his coffee cup. He put it down again. He stared hard at Martin, his eyes dark, promissory.

'He's an intensely private man,' Martin insisted. 'I know him well enough, but there are parts of his life he keeps strictly to himself.'

'Are you going to tell me,' McKaskill said, 'or are you just going to fuck about?'

Dermot stiffened a fraction but kept his face to the window. Martin looked at the carpet.

'I've thought this over,' he said. 'I just don't think I can do it. I don't want to do anything that would lead to Fletcher being hurt.'

'Who said he'd get hurt?'

Martin looked up.

'What else do you have in mind? A presentation? A surprise party?'

McKaskill pushed himself to his feet. He looked at Martin as if he might hit him.

'I don't have the time for this shit. I want that information off you and I want it now. You're not in a position to refuse me, in case you've been thinking you are. So out with it.'

'I think I *can* refuse,' Martin said.

He stood, returning the hard stare. This was a terrible risk, an invitation for McKaskill to escalate his malice, maybe even deliver some of it in blows. Martin could use his fists, but he knew he could never fight this kind of man.

'Tell me how,' McKaskill said, hardly unclenching his teeth.

'Your leverage isn't unopposed.'

'Speak bloody English.'

'I have my own leverage. I know a lot of people. Some of them are powerful, most of them are potentially dangerous in one way or another. I'm not defenceless. I have armour if I want it. Weaponry, too.'

'So you're a threat?'

'I can look after myself.'

'Bollocks.' McKaskill stepped forward and jabbed Martin's breastbone, precisely on the spot he had prodded the day before. 'Your ideas about yourself could get you up to the bumpers in trouble if you don't ditch them quick.'

'I think I'm realistic about myself, Mr McKaskill.'

'You reckon?'

Martin nodded. An angry smile twisted McKaskill's mouth.

'Look at this.' He stepped back, waved his arms to take in the entire room. 'This is what you are. Top show. Gloss. Sweet fuck all.'

'There's perhaps more to it than —'

'There isn't! You think you're this and that, all the bigtime stuff, a winner, right? Well, listen, Mr Martin Poofter Reynolds, you're nowhere. You're less than a dog turd if I decide you are.'

Something seemed to lock McKaskill's throat for a second. He coloured. Martin realised the man was close to choking with anger.

'You believe you're a dangerous kind of man, don't you? Dangerous and protected. *Safe*. That's how you've got yourself measured up.' McKaskill's eyes were like laser sources now, hot, darting dangerously over Martin's face and body. 'You're as safe as a mouse in a cattery.'

Martin watched McKaskill step back, appraising with tightly pursed mouth.

'The whole truth is, Reynolds, you're a big witless nelly that couldn't find his arse with both hands. And do you know how I know that?' McKaskill stepped close, his finger a fraction off the tip of Martin's nose. 'I know because you're one of the few men stupid enough to try standing up against me.'

Martin felt cool sweat on his spine. He glanced to the side. Dermot was still trying to be aloof, but his fingers were digging into the back of the couch.

'Are you threatening me?' Martin said, feeling he had to.

'Put it this way, I'm letting you know I can do anything to you I want,' McKaskill said. 'You and your bum-boy both. I could ruin you with one phone call.'

'I doubt it,' Martin said, full of regret the instant the words were out.

'Is that so?' McKaskill roared, making Martin and Dermot jump. 'Do you think I'm bluffing, then? Do you reckon it's bluff if I say I've got the goods on you and the high-and-mighty Mr Justice Inglenorth? The pair of you and a boy called Julian?'

Dermot glanced sidelong at Martin.

'I'm talking about the full goods,' McKaskill said. 'The fucking works — pictures, tapes, even a ten-minute video made near the judge's house at Dalveston.' He shot a glance at Dermot. 'Two years ago, lad. Before your time.' He turned to Martin again. 'That's all bluff, eh? Want to call me on it?'

Martin was devastated. The best kept secret of his erotic career, or so he had thought, was in the hands of this predator. He couldn't make himself doubt it. In spite of every elaborate precaution he and Johnny Inglenorth had taken, McKaskill had found out about them. His talent for espionage was phenomenal. Diabolical. And having made the discovery he would have gone all out to get graphic evidence, ruinous proof. It was his way.

'What do you say?' McKaskill demanded. 'Do I lay the claim and follow up with a Jiffy bag to the Home Office, or do you get in line and do what I've told you?'

Martin felt broken. It was as if his reinforcement had been pulled out, leaving him brittle and split.

Even so, he was curious.

'If you're so hot at getting the goods on people,' he said, 'how come you don't have a file on Mike Fletcher?'

'I never snoop near cozzers,' McKaskill said. 'They have a way of noticing. It's a nasty sixth sense lawyers and judges and other big shots haven't got. My two best men used to be cops — they're fucking mustard.'

Martin sat down. He clasped his hands and looked at them.

'Mike Fletcher has the third Thursday off in every month,' he said.

McKaskill stood nodding, willing the words out of Martin.

'He visits the cemetery at Olive Hill. Gets there about eleven o'clock.'

'What does he do that for?'

'His daughter died on the third Thursday of the month, at a few minutes after eleven. She's buried at Olive Hill. He spends ten minutes or so at her grave. I don't think many people know.'

'How do *you* know?'

'He told me one night when he was tipsy.'

'He goes on his own?'

'Always.'

'So he should be there day after tomorrow?'

'I would think so.'

McKaskill let out a slow, dry-throated sigh.

'Now that was easy,' he said. 'Wasn't it? Where was the need to give yourself all the stress?' He shook his head at Martin. 'I suppose it was your principles getting in the way, eh? You should forget principles and get yourself some good prejudices. They're a bloody sight more practical.'

Martin stood up. He didn't look at McKaskill. He went to the door and waited. McKaskill picked up the cup of half-cold coffee and swallowed it. As he put down the cup he looked at Dermot, who was staring at him hollow-eyed, visibly trembling.

'In case this doesn't get through to your protector in his present state,' McKaskill said, 'I'll tell you, so you can drum it into him later on.'

He came and stood close, so that Dermot had to look up at him.

'What he told me doesn't get him off the hook. He'll never be off it. And because he gave me a hard time, he just better hope I don't get a fit of spite one of these days and drop him in the shit, just for recreation. Tell him that, will you? Make him believe it.'

When McKaskill had gone, Martin sat down and cupped his hands over his face. Dermot sat opposite, motionless on the priceless couch, his eyes brimming with love and terrible concern.

TWENTY-ONE

Where was Percy Cullen? Where was his sidekick, DC Bourton? Why had Superintendent Foster left a message for Mike to come and see him as soon as he got back from lunch? Why had Martin Reynolds, visiting the station to speak with a fellow barrister on a drink-driving charge, deliberately avoided speaking to Mike? And who had whipped the CID day book?

It was the kind of afternoon when Mike recalled his theory that bloody-minded astral bureaucrats designed certain days to be fraught with puzzles and obstructions.

There were other mysteries in the station that day. Duggie Brewster, the desk sergeant, was processing some of them. What, he wondered aloud to Mike, had made a previously respectable architect's wife, with Women's Guild connections, decide to send poison-pen letters to a dozen honest citizens, her vicar among them? Why had a retired tea importer poured bleach into the petrol tank of his neighbour's car? Could anyone explain what drove a school teacher to make one of her young pupils eat chalk, then wash it down with ink?

'And what do you make of this one?' Sergeant Brewster flapped a charge sheet at Mike. 'A roofing contractor, fifty, former city councillor, arrested for throwing tiles at pedestrians from the roof of the public library.' He dropped the sheet on the desk. 'Is it all these food additives, or what? There's been a steady stream of nutters through here since I came on this morning.'

'Have compassion, Duggie,' Mike said, straight-faced. 'What we call madness is often seen as wisdom by the people afflicted with it.'

'I'll do that in copperplate and stick it on the bulletin board.'

'I don't suppose you've seen DS Cullen?'

'Not today.' Brewster shuffled his papers. 'That doesn't mean he hasn't been in — he might've been here all day, who knows? Skulking to the point of invisibility, if I may say so, is an art with some CID types.'

'How about the super — is he back from lunch?'

'Ten minutes ago.'

Mike moved off and Brewster called after him.

'Be careful. He's on a short fuse. I think it's his time of the month.'

'Cheers.'

When Mike entered the office Superintendent Foster was studying a map of the city tacked to his wall.

'Sit down, Fletcher. I'll be right with you.'

Mike sat by the desk and waited. Foster studied the map for another minute. He tisked and grunted a few times then strode to the desk. He sat down and snatched up the phone.

'Get me traffic.' He drummed the desk, not looking at Mike. 'Hello? Gorman? Superintendent Foster. I've been looking at the layout round the old cattle market — you know, down off the Derby Road . . . That's right. Have any of your units checked out that area? It's honeycombed with old sheds and warehouses. Worth a look, I think. Three-unit job, if you can manage it.' He paused again, listening, fingering his buttons now. 'Well, as soon as you can. And report back to me, whatever happens.'

He dropped the phone in its cradle, folded one hand over the other and raised his eyes to meet Mike's.

'So,' he said, 'we're still pursuing our solo career, I understand.'

'Who are "we"?'

'Don't be facetious, Fletcher.'

'If you'll promise not to be oblique. What are you saying to me?'

Foster's face churned. Around his eyes Mike read the lines of a long-term struggle to be taken seriously.

'This is an occasion for reprimand, at least.' he said.

'What am I supposed to have done now?'

'There's no *supposed* about it. I believe you spoke with Detective Sergeant Cullen in a public house yesterday afternoon.'

'That's right. I walked in on one of his recitals.'

'In the course of conversation you said you'd obtained evidence of irregular goings-on between Sergeant Lowther and Steve McMillan. You'd followed up on that evidence, you said, and you came to certain conclusions.'

'That's substantially correct,' Mike said, nodding. 'Your nark has a good memory.'

Foster flashed his version of a warning glare, which looked more like an appeal for Mike to lay off.

'You didn't mention the source of your original information, or the names of the people you subsequently interviewed. Further, you told DS Cullen that Sergeant Lowther was a sick man and wouldn't have lived long, anyway. You didn't say where you got that information, either.'

'I'm not obliged to make detailed reports to Cullen,' Mike said. 'He's a sergeant. I'm an inspector.'

'You're supposed to share information with other officers on the case,' he said. 'And you're *definitely* obliged to report any significant developments to me. You did neither. Why not?'

Mike recomposed himself in the chair.

'As for not sharing the information with Cullen, I did share it. I kept the sources to myself because I don't want a prick like him interfering with my informants.'

'Are you telling me you got your information from snouts?'

'No. Informants, I said. Not informers.'

'Then shouldn't the names of these people be put on record?' Foster tapped a book lying beside him on the desk. It was the missing day book. 'They're not in here.'

'They're not materially significant to my enquiries, that's why they're not in there.'

'I think I'm entitled to judge whether they're significant or not,' Foster said. 'Who are these people?'

'Just hang on,' Mike said, putting up his hand. 'Let me put the picture in focus. My reason for sharing the information with Cullen was to try and convince him we're looking for a victim, not an aggressor. I'd no great hope it would have any effect, given the man's nature, but you have to keep trying with these throwbacks, don't you?'

'You're avoiding my question.'

'I'm avoiding nothing.'

'Then tell me the names. The first one, anyway. I can guess where you got the medical information.'

'I don't think so,' Mike said.

Foster made a show of controlling his temper.

'The information about Sergeant Lowther's health was only made official this morning. You were in possession of it yesterday. That strange fact will be reported, Fletcher, and I'm sure the appropriate steps will be taken. Pathologists are no more immune from the rules of procedure than detectives are.'

'I didn't get the information from the pathologist.'

'Really,' Foster murmured, sneering bitterly at his desk top.

'Do I take it you're calling me a liar, Superintendent?'

'If you didn't get the lowdown from Dr Garrett, where else *could* you get it?'

'From Mrs Lowther.'

Foster looked like a man who had missed his footing on the stairs. He blinked a couple of times.

'Why did you interview Mrs Lowther?'

'I didn't. I had a cup of coffee with her, right here in the station. She talked about her husband's condition. He knew how serious it was, apparently.'

Mike could see Foster believed him. Lies hybridised with truth tended to work.

'What about your story that Sergeant Lowther was harassing Steve McMillan? Where did that come from?'

'Terry McMillan.'

'When did he tell you?'

'Yesterday.'

Foster got perhaps three or four chances a week to mime outraged authority, but it still wasn't convincing. He was too conscious of his image to be spontaneous.

'Yesterday?' he squeaked. 'Are you telling me you actually saw him, spoke to him, and didn't report it?'

Mike nodded.

'That's outrageous!'

'There was no need to report it.'

'He was wanted for questioning. Urgently. You should have brought him in, for Christ's sake.'

'You've got him tied down now,' Mike said. 'Has he told you anything?'

'That's not the point —'

'I know, I know. Foolish of me to forget that procedure overrides considerations of initiative and judgement.'

'Spare me your bolshie opinions, Fletcher!'

Mike sat back and folded his arms. Foster glared. Silence sat between them like a wedge. Finally the superintendent cleared his throat.

'I'll have to report this,' he said.

'Reluctant as you are . . .'

Foster leapt up and leaned across the desk, propping himself on his arms.

'In the privacy of this office,' he said, whispering hoarsely, 'I'll tell you now, Fletcher, that I don't like you. And here's something else — any chance I get to harm you, I'll take it.'

'Tell me something I don't know.' Mike stood up. 'Can I go now?'

'You can go when I say so.'

'Well, you better say so, because I'm going.' Mike walked to the door and stopped. 'Have you any idea where Cullen is?'

'Yes, I know precisely where he is. I know because he's an officer who keeps in touch, as he's supposed to do.'

'So where is he?'

'On the south side. He's following up a lead on Steve McMillan. He rang in this morning to tell me.'

'Who told him McMillan might be over the river?'

'A snout, I imagine.'

'He hasn't got any snouts.'

Foster waved his hand irritably.

'Whoever told him, he's following it up. He'll be back later this afternoon, I imagine.'

'Right.' Mike opened the door and paused again. 'Any theories about who duffed up Terry McMillan?'

'He had an accident of some kind,' Foster snapped.

'Like hell he had. He got a hammering, take my word for it. And here's something else to ponder — Terry's been in hospital since last night, but Cullen hasn't been along to grill him yet. Funny, that. Yesterday he was pissing himself for a chance to get hold of the kid. Now we've got him, he doesn't seem to be interested.'

Foster tilted his head.

'Just what are you saying, Fletcher?'

'I'm saying that when Cullen gets back here, don't walk near the fan. If you do, you'll get covered in flying shit.'

TWENTY-TWO

Guy McKaskill was working at the living-room table when Ella came down from her afternoon nap. She walked with the scissoring steps and side-to-side rolling of the chronic arthritic. Years of pain and over-eating had made her face grotesque. Lardy cheeks contrasted with sunken slitted eyes that seemed to ache. The skin of her face was tight and made her lips pout; they looked like two dried segments of tangerine. She paused by the table, looking down over her belly at the elegantly machined components Guy had spread out on a hand towel. He was polishing one piece with an oiled rag.

'What are you doing with that? I thought you'd got rid of it years ago.'

'Just you go and sit down,' McKaskill said, without looking up. 'I'll make you a cup of tea in a minute.'

He finished shining the gun barrel and put down the rag. One final time, for luck, he dropped the pullthrough into the end of the barrel and drew the wad of muslin along the four-inch length of the bore.

'There. All done.'

He thumbed the engraving on the barrel, SMITH & WESSON, to remove a tiny smudge, then deftly — he had practised it many times — he reassembled the weapon and laid it on the centre of the towel. He looked across at Ella, who had managed to lower herself into an armchair.

'Just keeping it clean. It's too good a tool to neglect.' He stood up. 'I'll put the kettle on.'

The doorbell rang before he made it to the kitchen. He answered it and found Sidney Pearce on the step, blowing his hands.

'Don't hang about, Sidney. I'm letting the heat out.'

Pearce followed McKaskill through to the kitchen, pausing in the living room to say hello to Ella and to eye the revolver on the table. Guy pushed the kitchen door to, nearly shutting it.

'So how's it all going?'

He filled the kettle and plugged it in, dropped teabags into three cups, put his back to the worktop and folded his arms. Sidney, as usual, avoided looking him in the eye.

'It's been a hectic day,' he said.

'I'm not here to hand out sympathy.'

'Administrative difficulties — nothing desperate, just tedious.'

The four o'clock update meetings were the closest Sidney ever came to feeling like a businessman. He took them seriously and tried, in the teeth of McKaskill's impatience, to conduct himself like a switched-on general manager reporting to his chairman.

'Mandy Chaudhuri got out of hand this morning. I had to read her the riot act. I think she got the message.'

'I never liked the idea of having wogs working for us,' McKaskill said. 'They don't think the way we do. I don't believe any of them really like us. They're permanent aliens.'

'But they know money, Guy. They respect it and they chase it like nobody else does. Mandy takes a lot of pride in her earning power. One Indian girl on the books is better than three white birds.' Sidney took a notebook from his pocket and riffled through it. He flattened it at a page covered in spidery figures. 'Eleven hundred quid plus, this month alone. That's what she's been worth to us.'

'And a lot of trouble besides.'

'That's just how she is,' Sidney said. 'It's in her blood. She likes to argue and find fault.'

'She likes independence, too. The wogs all do. I know you do spot checks, Sidney, but I'll still bet you that little brown cunt is bunging a percentage in the building society to launch her solo career.' McKaskill traced the pattern of the linoleum with the toe of his slipper. 'You know you said you read her the riot act?' He looked up. 'Any idea what that means?'

Sidney licked his lips, concentrating. McKaskill was always

doing this to him, pulling him up on things he said and asking him to explain them.

'Well, it means giving somebody a bollocking . . .'

'But why is it called reading the riot act?'

Sidney gave in. He shrugged.

'People do too much of that,' McKaskill said.

'What?'

'Use phrases and big words they don't know the meaning of.'

He was edgy, Sidney decided. McKaskill always got niggly when he was on edge. Niggliness on top of impatience could wear Sidney down very quickly.

'To read the riot act is a legal term. It means that when twelve or more people are rioting the magistrates have a duty to order them to disperse in the name of the Queen. The order's read in accordance with the Riot Act of 1715.'

Guy and his flaming encyclopaedia. He'd picked it up, ten volumes, at a bankruptcy auction. It was now his only leisure reading. He would sit with a volume on his knees and the rest piled on the floor around him. He soaked up facts for hours on end. He had turned into a know-all on some very odd subjects. Sidney recalled, bitterly, two hours he had spent in this house one night, dying for a drink while McKaskill lectured him on the legend of Saint Swithin, diffusion pumps and the history of enamelling.

'Anyway,' McKaskill said, 'what was Mandy Chaudhuri kicking up about this time?'

'The flat. She says we promised to get it decorated two months ago. The wallpaper gets her down, and she thinks it puts her clients off.'

'Bullshit. When a man's after a quick screw he isn't bothered about wallpaper. Did we really say we'd decorate?'

'We said we'd think about it. She went on about the bog, too. Wants a new one, new shower unit as well.'

'Tell her to go and jump a Turk. We've got — what? Eleven girls, twelve? Mandy makes more noise than the rest of them put together.' McKaskill sighed. 'You do things for people, you put them on good wages, hand out fringe benefits and bonuses, and the more you do for them the more they want to bugger you about. I hope you told her the consequences of me losing my rag, Sidney.'

'I think she's twigged it's no use trying to make demands.'

'Fucking right.'

The kettle was boiling. McKaskill unplugged it and filled the cups. He stirred them idly in turn, waiting for Sidney to go on.

'At eleven o'clock I tracked down Baxter and he told me little Davey's been picked up on suspicion.'

McKaskill stopped stirring.

'Where's Davey's stash?' he said.

'No worries, Baxter's got it. Fifteen ounces of Lebanese, sixty ten-quid deals of smack, some pills. The cops won't find anything on him. Davey's smart, he never carries for more than an hour at a time, and only when it's a definite sale.'

'He's smart, but he's under suspicion now. I think you should tell Baxter to ease him out for a while. Has Davey got a clean licence?'

'I think so.'

'Put him on driving, then. Six months.'

Sidney made a note.

'Anything else?' McKaskill said.

'The fags, whisky and brandy from the Luton warehouse job — we've got a promise of thirty-five grand for the rest of the consignment.'

'Who's promising?'

'Demarco Marketing.'

'Jesus Christ, Sidney . . .'

'No, no, hang on, Guy, they've made amends for the last cock-up. And remember, while they were at it they threw us two thousand for aggravation money.'

'But they're shaky. Italians are always shaky. They panic, those bastards.'

'So what? Even if they panicked enough to drop your name, where's the harm? There's nothing to connect you with that stuff, not once it's out of your lock-ups.'

McKaskill took the teabags from the cups with a spoon and dropped them in the pedal bin by the airing cupboard. He sugared the tea, added milk to his cup and Sidney's and stirred them. He worked with frowning detachment. He was edgy *and* he was distracted, Sidney decided.

'We want the money by Friday, absolute latest.'

'I told them next Wednesday would do, Guy.'

'Well fucking un-tell them. Friday or no deal.'

Sidney nodded. This was no day to argue.

McKaskill took through Ella's tea and a plateful of sweet biscuits. He came back and leaned on the worktop again.

'I wanted to talk to you about the books, Guy.'

'The books are my business, Sidney. Don't get above yourself.'

'No, no . . .' Sidney wrinkled his pointy nose, shaking his head. 'Not those books — the magazines.'

'Oh. Them.'

McKaskill had gone into pornography wholesaling reluctantly. Only the margin, never less than six hundred per cent, had overcome his resistance. An initial investment of ten thousand pounds paid out in Swedish kronor, yielded him profits of over sixty thousand pounds in four months. Even so the misgivings lingered, for there was a shame-troubled side to McKaskill's nature. He knew what those books were used for. In the trade they called them wank-mags. He disapproved of unmanly sexual habits. A man with a real woman, that was different, it was natural. As things stood he wouldn't handle homosexual magazines. There was a limit to what he would do for money.

'The magazines are fine, there's a good demand,' Sidney said, 'but a lot of the outlets are asking about videos, too. They're the big thing now. Bigger money than the books, now there's all the cheap Japanese blank tapes about. We can buy high-quality masters for a hundred and fifty a time and do our own repro work. The Swedes are quite happy about that kind of deal. For an equipment outlay of three, three-and-a-half grand, I reckon that with the distribution we've got, we could clean up.'

'Forget it, Sidney.' McKaskill gulped his tea. 'I don't want to go into manufacturing. Book import and distribution will suit me fine.'

Sidney shrugged. It was forgotten.

'Next on the agenda is the off-track betting,' he began, but McKaskill had a hand outstretched, waving him to silence.

'Skip the rest of it. I'm not in the mood. I want to talk to you about tomorrow.'

'Tomorrow?'

'Yes, the day after today, for fuck's sake . . .'

'OK, OK, Guy, I don't know what you've got on the stocks for tomorrow . . .'

'I'm going to get some justice for my son. His pound of flesh. Tomorrow.'

Sidney stared at the window, connecting the gun on the living-room table with McKaskill's plans for DI Fletcher.

'There'll be no problems, Sidney. But in case there are, you're my alibi. You and Baxter. I'll clue you, you clue Baxter, except you don't tell him what he's being expected to cover for. Got that?'

Sidney nodded. His face was troubled.

'Here's the story,' McKaskill said. 'Tomorrow, from twelve o'clock on, the three of us will be working on that white elephant of a car of mine. We'll be shut up in the garage with tools and flashlights and oil all over the place. It's set up already, the floor's a mess and there's three sets of greasy overalls. If anybody asks you later, you say we were trying to sort out the carburettors and fix the distribution, a whore of a job. It took us until dark, and still it wasn't right.'

'And me and Baxter,' Sidney said, 'we'll stay out of sight tomorrow, right?'

'There's hope for you yet, Sidney. That's right, you stay low. Go nowhere, see nobody. If questions ever *do* get asked, then my story, your story, Baxter's story and Ella's will all put me right here at home. The whole afternoon.'

'Fair enough,' Sidney said. 'I'll get right on to it. I'll track down Baxter and brief him.' He sipped his tea. There was too much sugar but he hardly noticed. 'Guy — don't fly off the handle with me, but that gun through there . . .'

'What about it?'

'Is it wise? I mean . . . *Guns*. They worry me.'

'That gun has no offical existence,' McKaskill said. 'And after tomorrow it won't exist at all. When I've finished with it, it goes through the crusher at the scrap yard, a piece at a time.'

'I can't help being worried, all the same.'

'That's your nature, Sidney. Old women worry.' McKaskill put his cup in the washing-up bowl. 'I'm not worried. I'm a bit restless, but I'm not worried.' He ran hot water into the bowl. 'Stay here and talk for a while. It'll keep my mind off things.'

'Want to chat about business, do you?'

'No, not business. Anything else at all, but not business.'

This was a stiff order. Sidney ransacked his brain for a topic.

'That new TV satellite's really something,' he said hopefully. 'Have you seen the amount of channels it carries? And imagine all that gold they've used to plate the reflectors. Bloody amazing . . .'

'Something else, Sidney. Talk about something else.'

McKaskill washed his cup patiently. He wasn't prepared to expose his ignorance of satellite technology. Like fish farming, computer science and AIDS, it wasn't in his encyclopaedia.

TWENTY-THREE

Life didn't affect Percy Cullen the way it affected ordinary people. At the age of eighteen he had begun to suspect he was special, a person who could read life's messages without deluding himself. As he grew older he got surer. Now he knew it with rock-hard certainty. He was able to see through smokescreens, to respond to the signal in any situation and detect a proper line of action. And however harsh the necessary action, however extreme, he could carry it out. Maybe it was a gift he had, a unique faculty — he didn't know, but, whatever it was, it flourished in him now and made his veins hum.

'It didn't take us long to work it out,' he said to the sweating man in the chair opposite. 'You burgled your own house, didn't you? You faked a break-in for the insurance.'

They were in an interview room at the station. After returning to the station and reporting to Superintendent Foster, Percy had come along to tie off this small loose-end, a case that had gone on long enough.

'The description of the man who tried to sell your father's pocket watch matches you to a tee, Mr Tainch. So does the description we got of the man that flogged your camera. It *was* you. You didn't have the sense to hide the stuff and hang on for a year or so before you tried to get money for it.'

'None of this is true,' Tainch said. His words were hollow, the vowels strung out. 'I couldn't do a thing like that.' He touched his thin moustache. 'I'm a religious man.'

'So was the last rapist I put away. Religion doesn't make any difference. Take a look round any prison. Christians everywhere.'

'But I simply wouldn't do it, I'd never dream of such a thing.'

Cullen let the reasonable expression leave his face in stages. He had nothing concrete on this man, only a hunch reinforced by an insurance snooper's report. Although Tainch's description roughly matched those given by the shopkeepers, they hadn't been able to pick him out in a line-up. There was no real evidence. So only a confession would do. Otherwise, no case. Percy's mouth stiffened.

'Don't mess me around, friend. Don't insult my intelligence.' He tapped the table. 'I know you're guilty and I've given you the chance to get this settled in a civilised fashion. If you think we should do things the other way, then we will.'

'I want to leave,' Mr Tainch said.

Cullen looked astonished.

'I'm entitled to. I've not been arrested, have I? I've not been charged.'

'You're obliged to stay here and answer my questions,' Cullen said. 'If you don't do that you'll be obstructing the course of justice, and you can certainly be arrested for that.'

Tainch looked very troubled. He fingered his chin.

'Is that true?' he said.

'As sure as there's shit in our cat. If you leave here before I want you to go, I'll have to come round to your house and insist you come back. If you refuse, you'll be arrested and put in the cells overnight, pending a charge.'

Tainch was swallowing it. He began to look trapped. That was fine. As soon as suspects believed their freedom was curtailed they started to wilt. Cullen fancied himself a specialist at handling wilting villains.

'But I keep telling you — I've nothing to confess.'

'Yes you have. And you'll sit on your arse there until it's out of your mouth and on to paper. That's my promise to you, Mr Tainch, my guarantee.'

This was all automatic, Cullen had done it hundreds of times. Today he was more detached than he had ever been. The breaking-down process trundled forward like self-propelled rolling stock.

'I want to speak to a lawyer,' Tainch said.

'What do you want to do that for? You haven't been charged. You just pointed that out.'

'Well, I . . .'

Tainch clasped his hands on the table. He couldn't think of what to say.

'I've got my pen,' Cullen said, holding up a ballpoint. 'And I've got a nice blank statement sheet.' He slid the paper forward and poised the pen over it. 'Let's get the job over and done with, eh?'

The door opened. Mike Fletcher stood there. Cullen frowned at him.

'A word,' Mike said.

Cullen sighed and stood up.

'Don't go anywhere, Mr Tainch. Stay in your chair. I'll be right back.'

In the corridor Mike pointed to the stairs leading down to the lockers.

'What's this all about?' Cullen demanded.

Mike walked ahead of him, striding briskly. They went down the stairs. By a table in the centre of the steel labyrinth, Mike stopped and turned to face Cullen.

'I'd like to smack your teeth in,' he said.

Cullen nearly made the automatic response — You and who's big brother? — but the reflex was stalled by Mike's expression. He was livid. In the shaded light of the locker room his eyes had a deep iridescence, metallic and threatening.

'Terry McMillan's going to be in hospital for a long time,' he said. 'Did you know that, Percy? Was it part of your grand plan for showing him who wears the iron glove around here?'

'What are you talking about?'

'I've just been to see him. They had to do an exploratory this morning, and all of a sudden it was emergency surgery. You didn't just wreck his shoulder and bruise his liver and bust a lot of muscle fibres on his stomach. You perforated his spleen, too. He could have bled to death.'

'What are you hanging on me?' Cullen shrieked.

'Are you saying you didn't do it?'

'Too bloody straight I am!'

'You did it, Percy. You're the one bastard of all the bastards in this station who wanted that kid bad. You were desperate to make the collar on his brother.'

'For Pete's sake —'

'And now it looks like you battered Terry for nothing.'

'This is crazy!'

'No arrest, I notice. Steve's still at large. You fucked up.'

Cullen tightened his red-and-yellow rugger tie.

'I'm not standing here and taking this. It's time the super got to know about you. You're off your skull.'

'Go ahead and lay your complaint. I'll be laying mine.'

Cullen hesitated. He had to know what Fletcher knew, if he knew anything.

'Listen, Inspector — I heard the kid was in a bad way and had to be taken to hospital. I *heard* about it just like you and everybody else did. I'd nothing to do with what happened to him. Why would I beat up a little bloke like that, for Christ's sake?'

'I already said why. You wanted to know where Steve was. But Terry either gave you a bum steer or he gave you nothing. That's not the point at issue — you did the job on the boy and one way or another you'll pay for it.'

'You're mad. Barmy.'

'Just see if I am.'

Mike pushed past Cullen and headed back to the stairs.

He had nothing, Cullen realised. *Nothing.* The McMillan kid hadn't opened his mouth. He knew better than to do that. Percy stared at the long row of lockers in front of him, feeling the exhilarating buzz in his veins.

In the corridor Mike saw the superintendent.

'Can I detain you for a second, sir?'

Foster stopped and glared at him, transferring his weighty folder of papers from one hand to the other.

'What is it?'

'I want to know what Cullen says he was doing all this morning and part of this afternoon.'

'I told you. He was following a lead on Steve McMillan.'

'Which presumably got him nowhere.'

'Every lead has to be pursued, Fletcher. You know that.'

'Sure,' Mike nodded. 'This one took Cullen to the south side, I recall you saying.'

'So?'

'So maybe he can move around without drawing too much public attention to himself, but he wouldn't go undetected by the south-side fuzz for more than ten minutes. Not one detective saw him or his car, no uniform men saw him either. I checked. He didn't report his movements to the South Division station, as he should have done. He didn't even have his partner with him.'

'What exactly are you implying?' Foster said sourly.

'Cullen was nowhere near the south side. He's been up to something somewhere else. I happen to believe that last night he beat up Terry McMillan. I also believe he's been conniving at some other nastiness since then.'

'And what fine set of instincts tells you all this?'

'My accumulated knowledge of Cullen tells me. My nose tells me. He smells all wrong.'

'You're talking like a bomb dog, not a detective.'

'This isn't a joke. Run a check on Cullen yourself. He's jangling. His vibes are out of kick. I'm telling you this now, I'm going to spend time making a case against that big bastard.'

'Now stop right there,' Foster said, and cut off, frowning at the desk sergeant who was running along the corridor towards them.

'Message just in, sir.' The sergeant's rubber heels squeaked to a stop. 'Number four mobile unit reckon they've found Steve McMillan.'

'Where is he?' Mike said.

'Machin's brewery. In the yard. He's dead.'

Mike stared at Superintendent Foster. The super tried to stare back. He saw the iridescent glint, the flaring anger.

'You'd better get out there, Fletcher,' he said, regretting he hadn't moistened his tongue before he spoke.

TWENTY-FOUR

It was dark when Mike and DC Chinnery reached the brewery. Men in donkey jackets and anoraks were erecting arc lamps in the yard at the back of the old building. A forensic team waited by the fence with cameras, ultraviolet scanners, miniature vacuum cleaners, brushes, collection bags.

Dr Garrett stood near the centre of the yard where the body lay. Beside him was his attendant, Albert Coker. Albert was holding the pathologist's scene-of-crime kit, a box with a stout carrying handle and black weatherproof covering. Inside were drawers with the items needed when the doctor answered a police call. There was notepaper, a pen and outline diagrams of bodies where the details of wounds on a corpse could be marked; there were two thermometers (two because they broke easily), disposable gloves, forceps, scissors, a magnifying glass, plastic bags to cover the hands and retain traces of blood and other matter, swabs, clean microscope slides, disposable syringes, a torch, a tape measure and a ruler for measuring wounds.

The arc lamps came on, flooding the area with white light. Mike and DC Chinnery crossed the yard and stood by Dr Garrett.

'Well then, Michael,' Garrett said, bending to look at the body. 'What do we have, I wonder.'

Steve had landed on his back. The bones of his shoulders and chest had broken with the impact. Fractured ends of rib and clavicle stuck out through skin and clothing; the upper part of the shirt and jacket were stained dark with blood. His arms and legs were at four different angles, the right arm snapped at the elbow. The back of the head was destroyed, the hair fanned out on the concrete, a corona of bloody bone fragments and brain splashed around it. The eyes were half open and blue veiled.

'How long do you think he's been here?' Mike said.

Garrett touched the left arm, moved it carefully.

'Quite a time. Rigor mortis is well established. Out here in the cold it would take a while to set in. The filming of the eyes, the flaking blood, the dirt that's collected on the brain tissue — all of that suggests the body's lain here for considerably longer than twelve hours. Nearer sixteen, maybe twenty.'

Mike chewed his lip absently, looking from the body to the scattered fragments of glass and rotten wood. He stared up at the dark window opening.

'He came out of there, then.'

Garrett nodded.

'Backwards,' Albert Coker murmured.

Mike and Dr Garrett looked at him. Albert was expressionless in his wisdom.

'Go ahead,' Garrett said. 'Fill us in.'

Albert put a hand to his mouth and rattled his chest a couple of times.

'The window's about forty feet up,' he said. 'Coming out frontwards, he'd have had time to go end-over-end just once. If he'd done that, he'd be on his back with his head nearest the wall. If he hadn't turned over, he'd be on his face with his feet to the wall. Coming out backwards they don't turn over. Not more than one time in a hundred. If he'd come through the window backwards and *had* turned over, he'd be face down, head to the wall. But he's on his back, feet to the wall. Backwards is the only way he could have come out.'

'What if he'd jumped and twisted in mid air?' Chinnery said. 'That'd put him in the position he's in now, wouldn't it?'

Albert's stare was part pity, part disdain.

'They don't do that, son. Leapers only leap out of windows they can stand up in. When they do it from that height, they nearly always hit the ground face first, or sometimes with their feet. There's a whole window frame here and it's not the kind you can open, never mind stand up in. Nobody dives through a window like that.' Albert coughed again briefly. 'The kid came out back first,' he said, 'and he sent the window down ahead of him. Excuse me.'

Albert stepped away a few paces with the bag. He put it down, opened it and started fishing out the items Dr Garrett would need.

'Is he right?' Mike asked Garrett.

'Probably. His mind's conditioned to forensic work. He's a sharp observer and his reasoning's neat. He's got nearly forty years' experience under his belt, too. If he'd been educated he'd have had my job off me years ago.'

Garrett took Mike by the elbow and led him to the fence.

'Have you a theory about what happened here?' he said.

Mike nodded.

'Can we talk about it? Later?'

'Certainly,' Mike said. 'I need to talk. The alternative impulse is to add another murder to your workload.'

'You're convinced this is a murder?'

'I'm positive.'

'Come to the mortuary in about an hour. We should be back by then.'

Dr Garrett crossed the yard to make his initial examination of the body. Half the forensic team worked around him, collecting fragments of glass and wood, taking dust samples, photographing the body and its position relative to the building and the boundary fence. Mike went upstairs with the rest of the team and looked at the tiny room where Steve McMillan had spent his last hours.

Later, back at the station, he shut himself in the CID office and rang Kate. He gave her only the bare facts — Steve was dead, he had fallen to his death from a high window. She was shocked.

'He must have been desperate. He wasn't a suicidal type. Not even remotely.' She listened to Mike's breathing on the line. 'How about you? How do you feel?'

'Terrible.'

'Stupid of me to ask.'

'There was no need for this to happen, Kate. I could have found out where he was. All I had to do was put a touch of pressure on his brother.'

'But you wouldn't have done that.'

'No, not with a kid, not ordinarily. But in this case, in the *circumstances* of this case . . .'

'You wouldn't have pressured the brother unless you'd known there was a chance Steve would die. And you couldn't have known that. So no self-punishment, huh? Promise me. It's the last thing you need.'

'I'll try to be rational,' Mike promised.

'Do that,' Kate said. 'Otherwise, you'll have me lecturing you on the harm done by internalised delusions of sin by omission.'

'Anything but that.'

'Will you be round tonight?'

'It might be late,' Mike said. 'Very late.'

'I don't mind. Come whenever you can. My back needs a cuddle. Desperately.'

Superintendent Foster, wearing his informal off-duty clothes — tweed jacket and cavalry twill trousers, ox-blood brogues, Viyella shirt, an umber cravat — brought the drinks from the bar and put them on the alcove table. He sat down opposite Percy Cullen and told him to drink up.

'Cheers, sir. Very good health.'

Holding his own drink a fraction from his mouth, Foster looked around the carpeted, amber-lit lounge of the Stapleton Arms. He approved. A safe, civilised, middle-class crowd used this inn. There was no stigma in being seen in such a place or among such people. Indeed there were advantages. Foster had received the first discreet offer of sponsorship to the Freemasons in this very lounge back in 1974.

'It might be a shade extreme to call this a council of war,' he said, turning his attention to Cullen. 'But it's as well to draw battle-plans before things go any further. Fletcher is out to make trouble for you.'

'I know he is, sir.'

'I want you to know you can rely on my support. That's why I've brought you away from your duties for half an hour — simply to give you my reassurances, and to confirm that we know how we're headed.'

'The DI seems to be obsessed with damaging me,' Cullen said, sadly bewildered.

'He's unstable in the head. His girlfriend could tell him that if she was any good at her job. I'm bringing up the matter of his attitude and conduct at my next meeting with the Divisional Heads.'

'Good move, sir. Best to get it done before the DCS comes back and saves his tail, like he's done before.'

'Quite. What I want to be certain of now, Percy, is that he won't spring any bombshells on us. Do I have your assurance that I'm not in the dark about anything?'

'You're completely in the picture,' Cullen said, husky with sincerity.

'This business about the boy, Terry McMillan — Fletcher's allegation is unfounded? I need to hear you say so.'

'It's completely unfounded. I was looking for the lad all right, but I never found him. Whatever happened to him, it was done by somebody else. God knows, he has enough enemies.'

'That kind always do.' Foster cleared his throat. 'I have to say, within the confines of this booth, that it wouldn't outrage me to learn you *had* given the little bastard a thumping. We don't sit down and reason with monkeys, after all. Sweet reason's for sweet reasonable people.'

'Absolutely.'

Foster sipped his whisky and frowned at the glass.

'One small thing . . .'

'Yes, sir?'

'Well, it's perfectly clear to me that Steve McMillan committed suicide . . .'

'And to me. It was on the cards. He was a nut-case, wasn't he? It's on his record. He was having sessions at the psycho clinic with DI Fletcher's piece.'

'Yes, but that aside — could Fletcher put a different slant on the case? That's something else we have to watch out for, isn't it? He could manipulate the circumstantial data. He could make it look, for instance, as if McMillan topped himself because pressure from our side was over-zealous.'

'He could try, I suppose,' Cullen said.

'We don't want to muddy the puddle with this stuff about Sergeant Lowther pressuring McMillan. But Fletcher might just want to do that.'

'He would love to,' Cullen said. 'It would suit his campaign to make Steve McMillan look like a martyr. He'd never come up with anything concrete, but he could get to the bleeding hearts in Administration. Another thing — he might put ideas in Terry McMillan's head.'

Foster thought about that for a moment.

'Ideas like changing the identity of his attacker?'

'Among other things.'

'Yes, I wouldn't put that past Fletcher.' The superintendent leaned across the table. 'Percy, whatever happens, take my word for it that DI Fletcher is going *down*.'

'It would benefit the force.'

'Amen. I've already told him I'll harm him if I can. And I will. It'll help if you get me some extra dirt on him. I can use all you come up with.'

'It'll be no problem at all, sir.'

TWENTY-FIVE

The tray carrying Steve McMillan's body rolled into the refrigerated chamber. Albert Coker closed the heavy steel door, sending an echo booming through the mortuary.

'I'll table the post-mortem for eleven in the morning,' Dr Garrett said. 'Don't come in till ten, Albert. You've had a long day.'

'Very good, Doctor.'

Garrett turned away, unbuttoning his overcoat, and nearly bumped into Mike Fletcher.

'Ah. I didn't know you were standing there. You move like a wraith.' He slapped Mike's arm. 'Come and have a coffee. I had the foresight to turn on the percolator before we left.'

They went to the office. The electric fire had been left on and it was warm. The aroma of fresh coffee hovered in the air. Garrett hung up his coat. He got two cups from a drawer of the filing cabinet and took the steaming jug from the percolator.

'A drop of brandy in it, perhaps?'

'I think so, in the circumstances,' Mike said. 'Are you still using the bottle of duty-free I brought back?'

'I'm down to the last inch.' Garrett poured the coffee and hoisted the brandy bottle from behind the cabinet. 'You'll have to make another trip to Lanzarote soon.' He checked himself at once. 'Sorry. We talked about that. No more Lanzarote.'

'I'm keen to give Tuscany a whirl, some time.'

'Don't delay, Michael. There's no place like it.' Garrett poured brandy carefully into the cups and recorked the bottle. 'One day in Florence will convince you. An hour in Siena will break your heart. Sugar?'

They sat with their cups, Dr Garrett at the desk, Mike in the deep chair alongside, savouring the coffee as the brandy warmed its way into them.

'This is a damned sad development,' Garrett said, broaching the reason for their meeting.

'It's a tragedy.'

'Most premature deaths are. I can think of only one or two that were actual blessings.'

'He was half of everything his mother had,' Mike said. 'I called in to see her on the way here.'

'Did you break the news?'

'I was spared that. A policewoman was there already. And a priest. They're hanging on, ready with comfort when the numbness wears off.'

Garrett picked up the notes and sketches he had made at the brewery yard. He studied them for a minute, then looked at Mike.

'Bring me up to date on what you've learned since the last time we talked.'

Mike repeated what Terry McMillan had told him about Sergeant Lowther and Steve, and he explained how he had satisfied himself it was true.

'Hours after he talked to me, Terry got himself beaten up. Badly. And then,' Mike concluded, 'only hours after that, if your estimate of the time of death is even half accurate, Steve was murdered.'

'Both attacked by the same person, do you think?'

'I've no doubt at all.'

'Do you have a suspect?'

'Yes, Detective Sergeant Cullen.'

'Heavens above.' Garrett displayed shock. 'Are you sure?'

'I think I knew it was him that sledgehammered Terry even before I went to the hospital.'

'This is astonishing,' Garrett said. 'He's not a man I've ever been able to like, but I never saw him as much more than a loutish bobby.'

'That's his base line. Lout. He's an accomplished bully, lecher, wife-beater. It's been said in his defence that he had a rotten start in life. Apparently he was brought up in an orphanage. Lots of violence and deprivation, you know the picture. But he made something of

136

himself in spite of the stunting background. I can take that into account, of course. But I can't use it to gainsay what he fundamentally *is*.'

'I take your point. Streptococcus can't help being a nasty bug — that doesn't mean we have to go easy with the antibiotics.'

'Anyway,' Mike said, 'I challenged Cullen, accused him to his face. He denied it, of course.'

'But you didn't buy that.'

'His behaviour was all wrong. It was amateur-dramatics innocence. Good liars can believe a lie while they're telling it. That's the way to make a denial convincing. Cullen was too deep-down pleased with what he'd done to Terry. He couldn't deny it to himself, not even for a couple of minutes.'

'Pleased, you say?'

'To a man with his outlook on the job, what he did was right. And it got results, so he was pleased.'

'And you truly believe he went to the brewery and killed Steve McMillan?' Garrett said. 'It's all very extreme, Mike. Was it personal? Was he a friend of Sergeant Lowther?'

'No. But it *was* personal. Cullen acted in accordance with his faith.'

'Meaning?'

'He believes implicitly in two precepts. One declares that criminals are irredeemable and should have no mercy wasted on them. The other affirms that policemen are inviolable. So his operating code's straightforward — keep the heel on the villain and smash him if he has the gall to hit out.'

'But killing? Surely his creed wouldn't stretch to that?'

'I could argue the point,' Mike said. 'But I don't think he meant to kill Steve McMillan. He most likely went to the brewery determined to duff him up before he arrested him. It went wrong. He lost control, went too far. Steve falling out of the window could have been an accident. I've looked at the remains of that casement — it's rotten right through.'

Dr Garrett got up and refilled both coffee cups. He handed Mike his and sat down again.

'What are you going to do now?'

'Since there's nothing I can *un*do, I want to concentrate on nailing Cullen.'

Dr Garrett considered the facts.

'You can probably do it,' he said. 'Young Terry will open up when he realises there's a chance of getting back at Cullen. His story will connect pretty obviously with what happened to his brother.'

'No,' Mike said, 'it would never work like that. It would be Terry's word against Cullen's. Imagine it. Here's a kid with a police record, plus a reputation for telling lies even when the truth would sound better. He goes up against a self-righteous DS who's marked for promotion and just happens to have the adoring support of his boss. Terry's story would be like a snow-ball chucked in a blast furnace.'

'The post-mortem, then,' Garrett said. 'If there was violence we'll find the signs. And there'll be the forensic technicians' results . . .'

Garrett tailed off as Mike shook his head.

'Cullen was missing this morning and for a good chunk of the afternoon. I checked out his yarn about where he was. It was horse shit. Tonight, when I went up to that little room in the brewery, I could see where he'd been, and what he'd been doing. Think about it. He had all night probably, plus most of the day.'

'Oh, dear . . .'

'I knew it when I looked at the floor. There was dust all right, and debris. But it was dust and debris that had been planted after the room was sanitised. Dirt that's been laid on doesn't look the same as dirt that's accumulated. The law of exchange won't be a factor in the lab results.'

'Nor on the body, I suppose . . .'

The law of exchange, the inevitable fact that a person entering a place leaves something there and takes something away with him, could be cancelled by anyone with enough time and motivation. Clothing fibres, dirt from the soles of shoes, smudges, hairs, fingerprints — all traces of a presence could be swept, wiped and washed away. The careful use of brush, vacuum cleaner and sticky tape rendered clothing and shoes innocent of proof that the wearer had ever been in a particular place.

'I can just see him,' Mike said. 'Cap, overalls, rubber gloves, plastic bags over his shoes, the lot. After he'd worked on the body, while it was still dark of course, he'd cover it with sacking and papers and other junk, just in case anybody looked over that fence before he was through.'

'Then, presumably, he'd go over every inch of the room, sweeping and swabbing,' Dr Garrett said.

'He'd do the stairs and the yard, too. Cullen knows the drill, he's read enough stories about houses and bodies that've been worked on until every trace of exchange is gone. I bet he even cleaned Steve's fingernails.'

Dr Garrett sat back in his chair, drawing grim conclusions.

'On the basis of what you say, I can assume all the evidence we find will be thin, a lot of it contradictory.'

'I'm afraid so.'

'Unless your sergeant's been careless.'

'He's never careless when it comes to covering himself.'

'Then he'll probably get away with it.'

'I'd like to think not.' Mike put down his cup and stood up. 'Can I have a look at the body?'

'Of course.'

They left the office and went along the darkened corridor to the tiled storage area. Dr Garrett swung open the chamber with Steve's name felt-tipped on the wipe-clean board on the door. He drew out the tray and put a trestle under the end. The body was still clothed and would remain that way until the autopsy, when each item of clothing would be carefully examined before it was removed.

'Is it all right to look at his back?' Mike said.

Garrett rolled the body on its side. A plastic bag had been placed over the head and secured at the neck; blood clots and brain tissue slid around the cavity of the bag as the head was turned.

'Can I pull out the shirt?'

Garrett nodded. Mike pulled up Steve's windcheater, drew the tail of the shirt out of the trousers and pushed it up, exposing tallow-coloured skin. He pointed to a dark bruise the size and shape of a bread roll, an inch below the margin of the ribs.

'That's what I was looking for.' He tucked the shirt into the trousers again and pulled down the jacket. 'Thanks, Doc.'

Garrett pushed the tray back into the chamber.

'What's the significance of the bruise?' he said.

'A kidney punch is one of Cullen's trademarks. He's been warned about it a time or two.'

'So?'

'I wanted to be sure. No, I was sure before. I wanted to be ultra sure. I needed the hard certainty of something tangible, visible. Now I've got it. Cullen did the deed, all right. He killed Steve McMillan.'

'Knowing it doesn't help you much, though, does it?'

'Oh, it does,' Mike said. 'It cancels my compunction.'

Dr Garrett stared at him, lost.

TWENTY-SIX

It snowed before dawn on Thursday morning. Martin Reynolds awoke at six to find himself alone in the bed. He got up to make coffee and found Dermot Calder in the kitchen.

'Couldn't you sleep?' Martin said, taking in the haggard, handsome face, the doleful set of Dermot's mouth.

'Could you?'

'Not very well.'

Dermot watched snowflakes hit the dark window and die away to droplets. Martin came close, put his arm across Dermot's shoulder and watched, too.

'This puts me in mind of lines from *Tam o'Shanter*.'

'What's that?' Dermot said, staring at the flakes.

'A poem. By Burns.' Martin recited quietly to the glass: '"Pleasures are like poppies spread: You seize the flower, its bloom is shed. Or like the snow falls in the river, A moment white, then melts for ever."' He sighed at the window. 'Black Thursday.'

'Yes.'

'I saw the Archangel yesterday, you know.'

Dermot looked at him.

'I did the cowardly thing, of course. Pretended I hadn't seen him, then hurried away.'

'I've been thinking about him,' Dermot said. 'Mostly I've been thinking about the other one. That horrible man, that monster. . .'

'Don't contaminate your mind.'

'It's not anything I can avoid. When I think of what he is. Vermin, he's just vermin, and yet he's in a position to take away everything from you . . .'

'Stop it, Dermot.' Martin spoke sharply, but there was no

coldness in his voice. 'Help me get coffee together. Fetch the cups and warm them.'

Dermot turned from the window and opened a wall cupboard. He tightened his jaw as he took out cups and saucers, fighting down a fluttering wave of fright. He hadn't the words to tell Martin how the very ordinariness of the kitchen, the neat calm that overlaid the house, made his sense of oncoming disaster so much worse from minute to minute.

He turned on the hot tap and waited. Martin was measuring coffee from the reservoir under the grinder. Dermot looked at him.

'Martin . . .'

'What?'

'You do know how much you mean to me, don't you?'

Martin looked up.

'Yes, I know.' He made a wry mouth. 'I wish you weren't so upset, old love.'

'I wish I'd no reason to be,' Dermot said, putting hot water in the cups.

In another part of the city Mike Fletcher was out of bed too, dressed already and taking tea to Kate Barbour. She had wakened early, heard him moving about, and couldn't go back to sleep. He kissed her cheek as he handed her the cup.

'You spoil me,' she said, and frowned at him.

'What's up?'

'You had a bad night. Chuntering and thrashing about. Is something bothering you?'

Mike shrugged.

'It's the case, I suppose.'

'That's what I guessed.' Kate sipped the tea. 'Poor Steve. I dreamed about him. He was talking to me, at last. Pouring everything out. There's a wish-fulfilling dream if I ever had one.'

Mike said nothing about his own dream. He had been sitting with Mrs McMillan, experiencing their terrible kinship, parents who had each lost a child. He had tried to soothe her with the consolations: she still had a son, and there was the chance of recompense for her loss, however waxen that might taste if ever she gained it.

'How about dinner tonight?' he said. 'My treat. We could go to the Italian place you like, whatsitsname . . .'

'*Rifugio d'Oro*. It's *molto* pricey. Are you sure?'

'I want to do something different, shake off all the gloom.'

'OK. I'll get myself tarted up for eight.' She grinned. 'I'm glad you suggested it. I've been feeling a bit jaded myself. It's time we both went out and ate too much and got pissed legless on Frascati.'

'Absolutely. And I promise I won't talk shop.'

'Hah! It'll be flying pigs, next.'

'Honest, I won't. You can do all the talking. You can tell me all about Jung's search for a soul, or about *Gestalt* psychology, it's time I wised up on that. And it'll be a chance to bring me up to date on the progress they're making on a cure for sex.'

'You're very lively this morning,' Kate said, aware it wasn't high spirits. He was tense, nervous. 'I don't think I can take it.' She pushed aside the duvet and swung her feet on to the carpet, balancing the teacup. 'I'm going to parboil myself in the shower. Then I'll make breakfast.'

'I'll brew a fresh pot of tea,' Mike said.

Kate suddenly remembered what day it was.

'Are you going to work today?' she said.

'For an hour or so. I've some odds and ends to deal with.'

Kate nodded and shuffled off to the bathroom, wondering what was wrong.

Cullen got to the station at 8.10. He signed on and went straight to the CID room. He broke step momentarily when he saw Mike was at his desk. Coughing to cover the small surprise, he made his way to his own desk. He dropped into the chair and glared at the duty sheet. Mike looked up, pushed back his chair and came across.

'I've been waiting for you, Sergeant,' he said. 'I want to make a statement.'

Cullen stood up, enlisting the advantage of his height.

'What would that be, Inspector?'

143

'Some time yesterday morning, probably very early, you killed Steve McMillan.'

Cullen tried to roll his eyes at this fresh lunacy.

'You might think you'll get away with it,' Mike went on, 'but you won't. I've put my suspicions in writing and later this morning the Chief Constable will read the letter. The least that'll happen is you'll get flung off the force. That's the *very* least.'

'I've had just about enough of you, Fletcher.'

'There's more of me to come.'

'Save it,' Cullen hissed. 'Just save it and blow it through your arse.' He squared up to Mike, jutting his chin. 'Here's a statement for *you*, while you're here.' He slitted his eyes. 'You're about to go down, friend, all the fucking way,' he said, paraphrasing words that had lingered near the centre of his mind since last night.

'If I do, you'll break my fall.'

'Piss off. You're pathetic.'

A tremor passed through Mike, the snapping of a wire kept taut for hours. Pressure released itself. His arms shot up and forward. One hand hooked in Cullen's hair and jerked him forward. His nose collided with Mike's speeding forehead. A knee slammed his testicles. Pain blinded him and fire blazed in his groin, making him roar. Both Mike's hands grabbed the rugger tie and tightened it, choking off sound. Cullen swung a huge arm and missed, gurgling, purple faced, and had the arm taken and twisted, wrenched until the tearing in his shoulder matched the inferno in his balls. Mike shifted his grip, taking a hold on the jacket lapels. He hop-skipped backwards, dragging Cullen with him, then brought his arms down sharply and smacked the sergeant's face on the edge of a desk. When he let go, Cullen fell sideways and on to his back. Mike bent and jabbed a punch on the gaping mouth, drawing blood.

He straightened and stood away. Cullen got to his knees, pulled at his tie until it slackened. He laboured to breathe, croaking obscenities like a man with his larynx torn out. He turned as he rose, supporting himself with one hand on the desk. His face was swollen and bleeding. His body appeared lopsided, as if its contents had shifted. Groaning, wheezing, he raised his hand and pointed at Mike. His rumble had the tone of a warning, but the words were garbled by blood and loosened teeth.

'Don't forget to tell Foster,' Mike said.

Without smoothing his hair or straightening his rumpled jacket, he turned and strode out of the room.

TWENTY-SEVEN

Davie Maguire's redeeming trait was that he never overestimated himself. He was forty, a shy man, lame from boyhood and facially disfigured by a mishap with delivery forceps at the moment of his birth. For nine years he had worked in a junior capacity to Albert Coker at the city mortuary. In that time Davie had learned to operate within his limitations and never tried to do things that were beyond him. Albert Coker recognised that Davie's slowness and frequent confusion couldn't be helped, so he accommodated them. Davie was aware of that. He was grateful to work under a man who not only forgave his shortcomings, but defended him from the harsher judgements of visiting pathologists and undertakers who found Davie's slow ways irritating or obstructive.

This morning he opened the mortuary at 8.45, as usual, and went round turning on lights and heaters. No bodies had been deposited overnight. Davie was glad of that. When the police and ambulancemen came in on their own, unsupervised, they upset the order that Albert Coker so punctiliously maintained. Davie had to re-stack trays, mop up blood, wash bootmarks off the tiles and, occasionally, clean the cups the police used when they made themselves a pot of tea.

In the kitchen there was a note from Albert: he wouldn't be in until ten o'clock. That was fine. It gave Davie time to dust in the office and make sure the toilets and washbasins were spotless and shining. He knew Albert liked to come in and find the place gleaming.

Coming out of the kitchen he heard a sound. The mortuary was full of sounds — the refrigeration motors, swing doors that creaked with the draughts, clanks and sharp clicks caused by dropping or rising temperatures within the chambers, the old ticking clock. They were part of the ambience, a steady and permanent background. The sound Davie heard was not one of those. It was an occasional sound, a creak and squeak, quite faint, near the front of the building. Davie believed someone had just arrived.

He went through and looked. The swing door of the alcoved entrance was moving, but there was no one in the office. He stepped nearer and looked through the glass panelling at the street beyond. There was no sign of anyone. But the door had been touched, opened, for it was stiff and never swung in the breeze like the others.

Davie went into the office. No, there wasn't a soul there. Yet he felt someone *had* been. What was it, what made him think that? He looked around him. The desk was tidy, the swivel chair in its usual place, the electric fire glowing now that it had been on for five minutes. *What was it*? He had been in here earlier and felt nothing was amiss. But now . . .

The back room, that was it. The door to the little cupboard-sized room where the safe was, where deceased people's property was kept, was half open. It was never left open. Shut, always shut. A panic flickered in Davie's chest. He went to the room and looked in. The safe was as it should be, squat and grey and locked. He tested the handle. Yes, locked tight.

He came out and closed the door. For a minute he looked round again, wondering. Unexplained things troubled him. It was hard enough getting through the day without mysteries cropping up. He tried to tell himself he was mistaken, the door had been left open by somebody and that was that. But what about the front door, swinging like that? And why hadn't he noticed the open door when he was in the office earlier?

He went back to the kitchen and sat down. The thing he wondered now was, should he tell Albert? He didn't like keeping anything from him. Albert was a straight honest man, direct and open, and he expected the same treatment from other people. He had told Davie more than once that if he had a problem, if he made a mistake or didn't understand something, he was always to come out with it. No secrets, no buried worries or doubts. That was the way Albert wanted things.

But what was the point of telling him about this? If he had been here, right now, he might be able to work it out. Fifty minutes from now, when it was all over and past, what could he do but worry? Davie knew how bad worry could make a person feel; it made him feel terrible, so why should he do that to Albert when there was no point?

He got out his dusters and went back to the office. Rubbing up the shine on the leather desktop, making himself busy — 'Busy's the best way,' Albert always said — he decided to put the mystery from his mind and say nothing about it. He would make himself forget. That wouldn't be hard. Upsetting as the puzzle was, it couldn't stay to trouble him long, for work always drove things out of his mind, and when they were gone they didn't often come back. The harder he worked the less he thought about. Davie liked it when he didn't have to think about anything.

TWENTY-EIGHT

'You look like you've been under a bus,' Superintendent Foster said. 'What happened?'

'Fletcher,' Cullen mumbled. 'He did it.'

He had waited thirty minutes in the superintendent's office, doing nothing to clean himself, determined that he should be seen as Fletcher had left him.

'Tell me about it,' Foster said, sitting down behind the desk.

'I walked into the office at ten past eight. Fletcher was at his desk. He was supposed to be off today but there he was. He looked up, came across and just went for me.'

Foster did small left-to-right scans of Cullen's ravaged face.

'I never imagined he was that handy.'

'I could have stopped him if I'd wanted,' Cullen said thickly. 'Bashed him crapless, come to that. But you wanted something on him. I reckon this is it, sir.'

Superintendent Foster looked as if he had been handed a prize he didn't want.

'It was just as you say? You didn't provoke him?'

'No, I didn't even speak. I'd just got in, like I said. He went for me. He's flipped.'

Foster appeared to have difficulty coping with this.

'But what the hell made him *do* it?'

'Mad people don't need reasons, sir.'

Foster drummed the desk with the fingers of both hands.

'Look, don't take this the wrong way — try to see things from where I'm sitting. A senior detective, a man I don't approve of but who nevertheless has a sound record of service, suddenly takes it upon himself to batter another detective for no reason at all. No *sane* reason, you say. Now that's going to be a hard one for the brass to swallow. Do you follow me?'

'I can't alter the facts,' Cullen said, wincing as one loose tooth bit down on another. 'He's just crazy — I mean, look at me . . .'

'I know I've agreed with you before that Fletcher's off-beam in his approach to the job . . .' Foster brought his hands together, let them fly apart again. 'I can't say he's ever displayed behaviour that would make me believe he could do this without some reason . . .'

The tight camaraderie of the night before was missing. Cullen, in his present embarrassing disarray, gave hints of some bizarre trick. Foster looked mistrustful.

'You've said yourself how disruptive he is,' Cullen pointed out. 'He does things to bend the works. What he did to me this morning, I'd say it's typical.'

'He's never done it before, Cullen.'

Not Percy, but Cullen. The detective shifted his feet, wary of the change.

'Where is Fletcher now?'

'No idea. He walked out.'

The telephone rang. Foster lifted it, identified himself. As the caller spoke he sat up in his chair. He nodded a few times towards the mouthpiece, looking at Cullen.

'Certainly, sir,' he said. He listened for a second. 'I couldn't say. He's officially off-duty today.' More nodding. 'Very well, sir. Eleven on the dot. I'll be there. Goodbye, sir.'

He put down the phone and folded his hands on the desk. His face had turned grave. There was no trace of the conspirator, only a superintendent confronting a detective.

'I don't know what's behind all this,' he said coldly. 'All I do know, or suspect, is that you haven't levelled with me, as I've continually asked you to do.'

'Honestly, Superintendent . . .'

'Cullen, is there anything important, very important, that you should tell me?'

Cullen swallowed.

'There's nothing, sir. I wish you'd believe me.'

Foster sighed and sat back.

'I have to see the Chief Constable at eleven o'clock. He's had a letter from Fletcher. It concerns you. He's made some pretty serious allegations.'

'Superintendent —'

Foster looked at the pleading eyes, fancying he saw fear.

'I have to tell you you're suspended, pending an inquiry. Go and get cleaned up and keep yourself ready to answer questions. Leave your warrant card with me.'

Cullen stared at the superintendent.

'They can't prove anything,' he said.

Foster stared back, showing him a face like a wall.

Olive Hill cemetery was on the south-eastern outskirts of the city. It was three acres of land at the top of a steep road, ringed round by irregular dwarf hills set with trees and shrubs. The place was old and well-tended, though nowadays few people were buried there. The preference was for cremation, and those who still favoured burial tended to book their last resting place at the newer, grotesquely landscaped Mount Drummond cemetery, which was easier for people to visit and had the additional advantage of a security patrol. Desecration was a hazard sensible people didn't ignore.

The snow had fallen steadily all morning. Now, just after eleven, it lay like a fine-woven sheet across the cemetery. Memorial crosses and angels stood out in grey and black relief, webbed filmy-white on surfaces exposed to the breeze.

Mike trod the muffled narrow path to the spot near the western fence where Moira was buried. He stopped opposite the small rectangle of granite with its cap of snow.

MOIRA CLAIRE FLETCHER

BORN 12TH DECEMBER 1972

DIED 17TH NOVEMBER 1988

Barbara had said the stone was austere. Mike didn't think so. It did its job: it was a marker and a reminder of whose remains lay there.

He didn't believe sentiments belonged on headstones. Too often they carried intemperate advertisements for the grieving of the bereaved, or extravagant claims for the saintliness of the deceased. Or, damnably, both.

Moira would have hated a stone with a verse on it. Or an angel. Mike had heard her say it, how indecent it was to decorate a grave with things like that. Might as well put gnomes there, she'd said; at least people could have a laugh at gnomes.

He stood with hands folded in front of him, looking at the softly indented oblong between the stone and the edge of the grass. He wondered why he kept doing this. Out of love? He loved Moira in his heart, he always would. There was no need to come to a cemetery to stand by a grave that contained not his daughter, but what was left when she had gone. It didn't soothe him to do this, it gave him no especial peace. Yet he felt, doggedly, that he should be here.

He looked at his watch. It was the time, almost exactly. The time on that final Thursday when her poor devastated body gave her up after ten days of progressive fever, sickness, prostration and eventual coma. The memory burned behind his eyes.

'Moira, my love . . .'

He looked up and inhaled sharply, feeling snow on his face. For that instant he knew, even if later he would doubt it: he was here because she would know where to find him, at this time if no other. And he would know where to find her.

Fifty yards away, hunching between two young trees that leaned inwards and touched each other, Guy McKaskill had a high, unobstructed view of Mike Fletcher.

'Stay there, now,' he whispered against the air. 'Don't move.'

He took the gun from the warm inner pocket of his padded jacket, thumbed off the safety catch and took a sight line along the barrel. Mike turned partly aside, presenting his back. McKaskill's chest swelled.

'Perfect . . .' he breathed.

An eye for an eye, a spinal cord for a spinal cord. McKaskill cupped his left hand under his right, propped his left elbow on his knee and steadied the gun. He put his eye to the rear sight and adjusted the angle a fraction of an inch. His finger curled close to the trigger, made feather-light contact.

Mike stepped aside sharply, went to the headstone and bent to brush away the snow. His body was behind a tree.

'Get back!' McKaskill hissed. 'Get back on the path!'

Mike moved further out of sight, only parts of his head and shoulder visible as he bent by a toppled flower vase and righted it. Then he disappeared altogether, carrying dead stems and leaves to a wire basket by the fence.

'What're you fucking *doing*?'

McKaskill felt the pulse drumming in his ears. His hand was still poised with the gun but it shook.

'Steady,' he commanded himself. 'Steady. Calm down.'

He thought of Derek lying in hospital and the connecting thought came — this chance missed, the boy's crippling un-avenged. That possibility wasn't to be entertained. Hot intent must prevail, there had to be reprisal. McKaskill's wrath was at its peak, he was as able now as he would ever be. Today was the appointed day, he had a belief in fateful times being crucially pinpointed. Another time he might miss, and if he did they would be on to him. Today he couldn't miss. All he needed was the chance.

'Come *on*, you bastard!'

Mike stepped back on to the path, brushing snow from his cuffs. McKaskill's eye came down behind the sight. Mike moved from side to side, shaking one shoe then the other.

'Stand still . . .'

The gun steadied at a tight downward angle as Mike's back turned to the muzzle again. McKaskill drew a deep breath and held it. His finger stroked the trigger. He adjusted the line of fire, aimed at a spot half-way down Mike's spine. His throat stiffened, locking in the air. Steadied, aimed, he tightened his finger on the trigger.

Flaring pain disrupted the moment. The trapped air surged from McKaskill's nostrils with a tearing sound and he fell back. He hit the snow and knew something serious had happened to his shoulder. Both shoulders. He felt another pain, stared up and saw a man bent over him, anonymous in a black balaclava and ski suit.

His arm flashed down. Fiery pain tore into McKaskill's chest. He tried to cry out and tasted hot smothering blood.

What is this?

His arms wouldn't work. He tried to hit the man and did no more than drop the gun. Tiny silver blisters of light peppered his vision. He needed to cough. He couldn't. The blood was like a warm river running from his mouth.

A thump between his legs flowered into the worst pain he had ever felt. It tore and blazed backwards, opening him, dividing his body. McKaskill felt a choking surge of blood in his throat. It forced its way out of him and he knew nothing more.

Dermot Calder stepped back from the body. He had never seen so much blood. Miraculously, none of it had gone on him. It stained the snow all around McKaskill. It trickled, steaming and sickening, from his mouth and groin. He looked dead, even though his blood looked so lively.

Shaking, but still in control of himself, Dermot dropped the yellow Stanley knife on the snow and rubbed it back and forward with his boot, washing it spotless clean. He put it in his pocket, bent low over McKaskill and decided he was gone. Carefully, cautious of jellying blood on the ground and on the clothes, he took the arms and dragged the body back into the cover of the two small trees. He stood then, taking a last look at the contorted dead face, knowing that under his agitation there was relief, the most blessed relief he would ever know.

He glanced down at the cemetery. The Archangel was still there, standing motionless by his daughter's grave, his coat collar up. Dermot turned and made his way back down the hill. He climbed on to a wall by a dirt road and sat there. The big snow boots came off easily. He dropped them on the ground, took a pair of green trainers from inside his zipper jacket and put them on. They were reassuringly warm on his feet. He pulled the balaclava tightly around his face, jumped down on to the road and picked up the boots. They were new but he would burn them, burn the trainers too.

Treading the snow-choked verge towards the main road he tried to picture a future scenario. McKaskill found on a hill overlooking a cemetery, mutilated and dead, beside him a gun with his prints on it.

Dermot tried to see trouble in that picture, and decided there was none. Nobody could imagine that he, an aesthete, a dancer of delicate sensibility, could butcher a dangerous criminal and embellish the slaughter with a symbolic castration. McKaskill was a bad man, known to be bad, and the assumption would be that he had fallen foul of his own kind.

Furthermore, thought Dermot, who was to draw any serious conclusion from the fact that the Archangel's daughter was buried down in that cemetery — even if it became known Fletcher had been there, even if anybody could work out that McKaskill had died that same day?

The Archangel was saved from terrible harm, maybe even death. That was what mattered. Martin was safe now, too, which mattered even more to Dermot.

He reached the corner and turned right, down to where he had left his bicycle chained in a clump of trees. As he walked he wondered at how calm he felt, how untroubled by what he had done. He believed he would suffer no remorse over this, no bad dreams. Killing the man had been nothing compared to the fears he'd had for Martin.

Dermot walked briskly now. The toughest thing, he supposed, would be to keep himself from telling Martin what he had done. But he would never tell, whatever the temptation. The last thing he wanted was for Martin to be frightened of him.

TWENTY-NINE

The snow swirled thickly as Mike came out of the cemetery. He stood by the gates and adjusted the lapels of his coat, folding one over the other, holding them in position because the retaining button had gone. He glanced over his shoulder, assailed by a sense of leave-taking, then turned and walked off down the steep road.

The flurrying particles seemed tuned to his feelings. The visit had made him hurt, as always. It was a small rage in him, a cut-loose directionless part of his spirit that ran in circles, knowing it could never find what it must search for, regardless. Coming here made him feel lost to any warmth.

He would feel better, of course. An hour or so would do it, make his hurt manageable. Until the next time he came.

He quickened his steps, planting his feet carefully to keep from slipping on the snow. Rounding the corner at the foot of the hill, he brushed snowflakes from his hair and looked at his watch. It was 11.28.

Things would be happening. The Chief Constable would be acting on the letter, having no option. Cullen would be put on suspension. Two senior officers from an outside force would go to the hospital and interview Terry. He would talk. Before coming to Olive Hill Mike had visited him and explained that the threat was gone. He could tell his story and have something done about it.

And the post mortem on Steve would be underway.

Mike thought back over the morning and got a mêlée of sensations, mostly precarious. Breakneck plans took small account of risks, which was just as well. His assurance had held. Thumping Cullen had been easier than he'd thought, because the sergeant's manner had been a perfect goad.

After that, things hadn't been so straightforward. He had felt queer, covertly unbalanced, sticking his hands into his jacket pockets and simultaneously into polythene gloves. He had walked out of the station like that. Out of the station, into the park, and then a quick dash to where the trees opened on the high rear wall of the mortuary yard. The keys hadn't been a problem, they were always on the hook at the station, for use when the mortuary was closed and a body had to be deposited. Mike had lifted them first thing, he would put them back before the day was over.

So he had let himself into the mortuary yard and thence into the main building, locking gate and doors behind him. At 8.23 by the big clock, he had rolled Steve McMillan's body from the chamber and set about reinstating the law of exchange.

It had been tricky. His hands had sweated in the gloves and particles stuck to the plastic. He had to turn the gloves inside out, then hunt around for tweezers to pick off hairs, fibres, a fragment of the underside of Cullen's jacket lapel. The bags were removed from Steve's hands and, painstakingly, the evidence was transferred: hairs between his fingers and under one nail; a fragment of skin — a surprise find — was pushed under another nail; red and yellow fibres of rugger tie were put on the windcheater and in the curled palm of one hand; a smear of blood punched free from Cullen's lip was dabbed on the shirt and one cold cheek. There was more on Mike's hands, a sweated collection of flecks and speckles, plus something gelatinous gained from the head-butt and wiped away on the back of his wrist. All were transferred to Steve's hands, to his face and clothing, liberally and with fervent intent.

And then Mike had nearly been caught. The body was put away, the light turned off, he was on his way back to the office with the tweezers, when click! a key turned in the front door. He made it into the poky room beyond the office and stood there, cramped, bent half-way over the safe as Davie Maguire limped in, put on the electric fire and moseyed out again. It dawned on Mike now that he had left the door of that little room open. No matter, he decided.

In view of their discussion of Cullen's clean-up job, Dr Garrett was bound to wonder. He would scrape fibres, swab off blood and dried goo, dig out hair and skin from under Steve's nails. He would put them all in bags for the lab and he would certainly wonder. Could he accommodate the belief that Mike Fletcher was a man capable of planting blood and snot and fibres on a dead body — that he was capable, in God's name, of beating somebody up to get hold of such stuff?

Again, no matter. At best, the doctor would regard the evidence as good fortune, a crazy oversight of Cullen's. At worst, he would harbour a suspicion on which he would make no comment, take no action.

The rest of the day would be a pain. Mike would have to talk with the Chief Constable, there would be yards of questions and a report to write. Before all that, before the necessary tedium, he would drop by the mortuary and have a dram with Dr Garrett. A couple of drams. He would do his best not to make it look like he was celebrating.

He stopped to brush snow from his hair again, and had an involuntary vision of laughing, sunny-haired Moira. It was a fleeting epiphany: she was real, closer to him than the chill reality of the street where he stood.

Crossing the road, he decided to treat the passing sensation as a sign: he *had* been close to Moira today, to whatever essence of her survived the baffling business of being alive. The pain he'd brought away from the cemetery began to fade. In its place a sweet melancholy was gathering, the kind that deserved encouragement.

He glanced across the pavement and decided he would have a couple before he got to the mortuary. Going through the door of the Fox and Hen, he realised he was nearly smiling.